Murder Most Fowl

A novella
Written by S. G. Lee
First Edition 2016

SB

An imprint of Shillelagh Books
London, Ontario, Canada

Acknowledgments:
Sincere thanks to Jodi and Sydney, without your constant support and encouragement, this book would not be possible. You are the best friends a writer could have. I dedicate this book to my daughters, my son-in law and my husband; who have supported my writing endeavours with encouragement and love. Special thanks to my beloved mother in heaven, who taught me dreams, can come true with hard work, perseverance and patience.

Table of Contents

Preface: A Note from the Teller of Tales

D o ever wonder what makes people tick? There are all kinds of murders some more fowl than foul.

Have you ever wondered what makes people suddenly snap and kill someone? What justification anyone can have for murder? I caution you that these murders will shock you, but you may also find yourself cheering the murderer on.

Read on dear reader if you dare and see if the defence and the rationalizations this people make sense to you in these thirty four stories.

What are you waiting for turn the page and begin...

Murder Most Fowl

T he man walked into the room and looked stern as he commented, "She seems taciturn and uncooperative."

"Should we hose her down?" asked the woman.

"At least it would get her cleaned up. She's a mess."

"I can't believe she did this. She's never done anything like this before," the woman complained.

"There's always a first time."

"You have to give her credit it was creative."

"Yes, murder most fowl. Ha, ha. How many eggs did she crack?"

"A dozen. She said she did it for her art."

"So we have a five year old, little artist in the making?"

"Looks that way! But I'm going to keep my eye on her," replied her cop father.

~0~

It wasn' t my fault

It wasn't my fault. I know all murderers say that, but it really wasn't my fault. I know what you're thinking, how is that even possible? You want me to explain, but it's a long story. What is my name? Amy. That's all you need to know right now.

What you have the time for a long story? Well if you insist, I'll tell you my tale but don't say I didn't warn you.

It all began when young. You understand when you first go to school and everything is new. Most people when they go to school experience new friends and wonderful experiences, but it wasn't that way for me. I felt left behind, as I started in grade one, not kindergarten and everyone knew everyone else, but not me. Everything and everyone was strange and alien to me. I had to be quiet and listen to this stranger at the front of the class. I was told to do sums and read; but all of this was too easy and I was bored. The teacher noticed I had finished my work and allowed me to go play with toys at the corner in the back of the room. I lifted my hand and toys danced. I thought everyone could make objects move so imagine my surprise when I was met with stares of disbelief and some disgust and fear.
I was asked how I could do such trickery and when I said I just thought it, the teacher sent me to the corner. I begged to know my transgression but my teacher just shook her head and banished me in the corner for hours.

What does any of this have to do with my present predicament you ask? That manifestation of actions from thoughts appeared the beginning of my powers, which only increased as I got older. I had the ability to manipulate objects and read minds. I could see the tests results in my head and couldn't shut it all out. The voices were getting louder as well. What voices you ask? The little voices that people have in their heads which multiplied by every head in the school. I had trouble shutting them out, so much so that I suffered headaches continuously, until I created a door in my mind with many doors to shut each voice in.

Did I tell anyone about these new found powers? Are you kidding? They'd called me magic girl since grade one and I didn't want any more attention brought to me. Some actually believed I used magic tricks to make things move.

I soldiered on and tried to adjust to these new powers as they came. Most of all I tried to hide them. I was fourteen years old, socially backward and awkward and totally in love with my crush, Stanford Remington. Nearing Valentine's Day I knew there would be a dance. Something called a Sadie Hawkins dance where the girls ask the boys to the dance. I wanted so bad to dance with him

Stanford was the handsomest boy in my class. His blonde wavy hair and blue eyes were so dreamy. I fantasized being his girlfriend and having him walk me to the dance. I was in love with him, but was he in love with me? I wanted to ask him to the dance so badly. I hesitated and took days to make my move and ask him to the dance.

As I approached Stanford, I saw Heather and Marisol whispering in the corner. A few minutes before they had been talking to Stanford had one of them beaten me to the punch and asked Stan out?

I stammered and took a huge breath to begin again finally squeaking out a request for Stan to go to the dance with me. We went to the dance and that was the start of Stan and Amy. Ha, ha you thought I'd say I went all Carrie on him. Didn't you? No, that's not how it went.

Stan popular with all, I felt the need to be the same; so I hid my gifts to fit in. My high school years were magical as Stan was the quarterback and I became the head cheerleader. Okay, so I used a little of my gift it's not easy to balance on top of a pyramid you know.

I was happy, truly happy when I went off to college for the first time. I enjoyed the courses and got all A's in advanced mathematical courses and of course Physics. I dated Stan still and he oozed sweetness and charm. He said we'd get married as soon as we finished school and had given me a diamond solitaire engagement ring. Then I found out I was pregnant. I had missed periods, but since that had happened before, I didn't put two and two together. Only the slight weight gain alerted me. I was nineteen years old and seven months pregnant already in my last year of college and I could easily finish before I gave birth. I had been offered jobs all over the country after graduation. I determined I would tell Stan and we would be married before the baby was born.

Looking forward to telling Stan the news and knowing he would be as happy as I was; I went to find him. Getting to talk to Stan the day I found out, was next to impossible. He dismissed me on the phone saying he had to go to a party that night at the sorority house. I insisted I urgently needed to talk to him. He said he loved me, but I'd have to wait he'd promised to go to a bachelor party at the sorority house this evening. I said I would wait in his apartment then we could talk when he came home.

I went to the apartment. I watched some television and then tired; I fell asleep. When I awoke, morning sunlight filled the living room and there was no sign of Stan. Stan was the kind of man that always called. Worried I called everyone I could think of, but no one had seen Stan. I called the police and they found him dead at the sorority house. An overdose of alcohol had killed him. When I got the story of how he died, rage grew inside me. I felt it built and felt the air move around me. I struggled to regain control but it was impossible after I found out how he had died. Three of his so called friend had held him down and poured alcohol down his throat with a funnel. Stan had passed out and later died after they'd left him there.

I went to the morgue to see him. He looked as if he could be alive, that any second he would kiss me; but when I touched his lips they were cold and his skin icy too. A fiery rage grew inside me, one like I'd ever felt before. I thought how my baby would never see his or her father. I felt the kick and the fury from my baby, as she read my thoughts. I knew she too was angry.

I felt the power that resided within her tiny body more of the ability than I had in myself and I grew afraid for her. I vowed I would protect her and keep her safe at all costs.

I arranged the funeral with the help of his mother and told her of our child. She said it was bittersweet that she would have a grandchild, but lose her boy. We consoled one another and she invited me to stay by her side at the funeral the next day.

They came then, the two of them…murderers with sympathy and cards of condolences. Those two so-called friends Charlie Tappets and Angelo De Marco,(the third friend Harold had disappeared.) They were all smiles and solicitation and my rage grew added with my child's own. Why weren't they in jail? Why didn't they suffer? Our rage grew and entwined, exploding out of my body striking them dead on the spot. People looked horrified all thinking something behind me had given off sparks that struck them.

The funeral director started CPR, but the two of them were dead as doornails. The police came and ruled that a spark from a nearby outlet and had surged and killed them, but I knew that my daughter and I had got our revenge. It wasn't my fault. I knew I had allowed my rage to takeover and used her power with mine to kill them, but I wasn't even aware we had that power. It truly wasn't my fault. I knew that but I was afraid for my unborn child and the power I wielded I decided I had to keep everyone safe from the gifts Lee and I had.

There was no taint on my unborn child; but I felt we needed to get far away from people. I had to take her somewhere safe. Somewhere that I could teach her how to control our gifts and maybe in do so learn how to myself. After she was born we moved away far away on a research station in the pacific. It was the only way to protect my daughter Lee and the world from us. My daughter is a young woman now and she moved away to go to college and see where her father died. She knows the extent of her power and she knows how to control them all. At least I thought she could; but absolute power can be an uncontrollable thing. Emotions can be unleashed that can harm.

It wasn't my fault I let her go and the sorority college burnt down. It really wasn't my fault or even Lee's. The wiring was old after all and the sorority... well they shouldn't have had Charlie Tappets and Angelo De Marco picture so predominant in the foyer. No one died, or so they said at first, after all the building was an old foolish sorority that should have burnt down years ago. So it wasn't really my fault, when they found Harold dead in the sorority ashes. Harold had taken a job there you see, out of guilt for his part in Stan's death. Too little, too late. Revenge had killed him justice was served. How could I have known that Lee would find him there and the rage would get out of its cage? Or she would borrow my power and to add to hers to end his life?

Yet I still I comforted Lee. She grieved for what we had done with this great power. I took her in my arms and let her cry when she confessed what she had done.

I put on the kettle and poured the drinks in fine china cups. I then offered her a drink and she drank deep of the tea. I drank deep of mine.

"I know, mom," Lee admitted," in her last breath," I know and I forgive you."

So you see I am a murderer. Lee is dead and I will be too within the next few minutes, but it wasn't right for us to live in this world. We can't control our power. We lied to ourselves that we could, but the world wasn't safe while we were alive. So you see it wasn't my fault, I didn't lie. For absolute power corrupts absolutely. And now it's time to say… Goodbye ~

~0~

Nothing Personal

Stephen woke up and looked around. He couldn't believe he'd been grabbed from his bed and brought here to the warehouse. The place was dank and dark. Who had brought him here and why? Stephen became more aware now found himself tied to a chair waiting for what? His demise? Plastic sheeting was beneath the chair and he grew afraid.

Stephen once again looked around and spotted Stevie watching him and another muscle man and the boss.

"Why?" Stephen asked.

"It's nothing personal, kid."

"Nothing personal? I didn't do, no matter what they say I did."

"Even if I believed that, I could do anything about it. I have orders from the boss."

"I thought you cared about me."

"The boss tells me what to do, and I do it's that simple."

"So you'd kill me?"

"With regret I would; but if it comes to my life, or yours, simply put mine is more important."

"I can't believe this. Mom always said you were no good and I shouldn't get mixed up with you."

"Maybe you should have listened, boyo!"

"Can you handle this on your own, Stevie?" asked the boss stepping in, "I've been called to Chicago."

"Sure thing, boss."

The boss then left taking his henchman. Stevie untied the ropes around Stephen. He marched Stephen out at gun point in front some the other men waiting outside. Stephen trembled with fear but he didn't want to give Stevie satisfaction so he tried to hide it. Stevie then motioned for Stephen to get into his car.

"So you're not going to kill me?" the man asked when they entered airport parking and went into the airport.

"I convinced you? Good, then the boss will believe."

"I thought I was a goner. Where can we go?" asked the young man.

"We're going to South America. No matter what your mother said, God rest her soul, I would never harm my own son," the man answered, picking up tickets at a kiosk, "We're off to Buenos Aires. I bought a place there years ago, for my escape."

"But I need a passport."

"Check my coat pocket."

"Wow, you think ahead, Dad."

"Always stay a step ahead, son. That's why I forbid you addressing me as dad in their company. None of them know you're my son. They think it's a coincidence we have the same name."

"We have time to get away?"

"I've planned everything Stephen' by the time they realize I'm gone and I didn't kill you, it will be too late, for them!"

"What do you mean too late for them?"

"The FBI will be rounding them up. I left a sworn statement as well as video tape. They will have evidence that they killed me and you."

"But they didn't kill us," Stephen protested.

"That doesn't matter the courts will think they did. That should keep them from looking for us."

As the men sat down in their airplane seats they breathed a sigh of relief. They were on the plane and in the air; off to their new home and away from the mob boss. They were truly safe.

~0~

His Obsession

It happened so fast, in the blink of the eye my life changed forever, but I'm getting ahead of myself. I thought my life was happy; I had a good job, a good marriage and the prerequisite two children, a boy and a girl. I was blessed and didn't even know. I hugged my husband and children, got into my car to go to work, and to all intents and purposes disappeared. What really happened was a whole different story, then what everyone read in the papers.

I drove along oblivious to my surroundings my mind on whether my boss would like my presentation, about how I needed to pick up a present for a birthday party my daughter Ivana would attend; when I felt a poke in the middle of my neck.

"Pull over lady!" a voice came from behind me, "And don't turn around."

I wondered why, oh why, hadn't I checked the backseat of my car? Why hadn't I been so fool hearted about my own safety? Why couldn't I have been careful? The voice was deep and sounded familiar, but fear gripped me, as I realized that gun poked in my neck. My mind raced trying to find a way out.

Cooperation seemed the only way, considering the weapon.
But when we got to where ever he made me go I'd attempt
an escape. Why hadn't someone kidnapped me? I wasn't a
beauty. After two children I had gained weight and
bordered on chubby. Okay, I'm lying, I was fat. I weighed
over one hundred and sixty pounds and I was five feet five
inches tall. I did think my long brown hair, which was
feathered in waves to frame my face, appeared lovely, as
were my brown eyes, but I feel most men didn't really look
at fat me.

What was wrong with me that I had gone from been
terrified, to wondering if this perpetrator thought me
beautiful? I didn't care, if he thought me beautiful; I just
wanted to have him, let me go in one piece. What did he
want me from me? It had to be a case of mistaken identity, I
reassured myself. He'd let me go once he found out.

"Please don't hurt me. I have two young children," I
pleaded

"I would never harm you Natalia," he said soothingly, his
pronunciation of my name caressing and over familiar, but
somehow this creeped me out more.

He knew my name this wasn't a stranger pickup he knew
me. What did he want of me? Who was this in my
backseat?

The voice sounded so familiar, I racked my brains trying to
remember where I heard it before.

"I'm hurt. I'm really hurt that you don't recognize my voice."

"Alexander? Why would you hold a gun on me?"

"I didn't know whether you would cooperate and I needed you to come with me," he commented and then laughed.

"But I thought..."

"You thought I was dead?"

"You know I did. I loved you how could you?"

"Natalia, I couldn't tell you. I couldn't tell anyone."

"We were married and I was pregnant with your children, our twins."

"You moved on quickly enough with him," Alexander reproached.

"He was there for me. I was pregnant and alone. Where were you?"

"I was in a hell hole thanks to him."

"Thanks to who?"

"Your husband, that's who he is now! Isn't he? Except you are still legally married to me! Quite a quandary, wouldn't you say?"

"You're saying Jack did something to you? Jack doesn't even know you."

"Jack knows me," he laughed then continued, "Jack is my cousin.

"Are you delusional, or just obsessed with me? This sounds ridiculous. Jack has no family."

"I wish Jack had no family. Jack told me that with a flick of his fingers he could take over everyone and everything in my life He said that if I made it out of that hell hole he had me thrown in, that you would never believe me."

"You're lying! Jack has been there for me. He was there when the twins were born. He's a great father to them!"

"My children!! Not his! He took them too. I'm sure he's kept you but saying things like. I love you, but you could stand to lose some weight. Don't you think that color is wrong for you?"

I realized that Jack had said things like that to me. I started to waiver and wanted to believe Alexander, but I also knew my former feelings for Alexander could betray me.

"That's what a good husband does," I insisted.

"I didn't. I would have said you were lithe and beautiful, with an edgy, iconic style, all your own. That after all these years you remain, the most stunning woman I've ever seen."

"You weren't around long enough to say anything that nice, or as constructive as Jack did."

"You call that constructive? Natalia, you should be glad I've come to rescue you. You deserve compliments every day and kisses that leave you breathless and wanting more."

"You need help Alexander. This is all in your head. We're over by your own hand. Faking your death was cruel; don't think you can woo me to your side with flower phrases. I've moved on you should too and claiming Jack is your cousin is the last draw..."

"Pull over. I can prove he's my cousin."

I pulled over the car. I couldn't believe that the love of my life was alive, let alone that he claimed my husband, Jack had orchestrated the whole thing. I didn't trust the story I heard, but I could hear Alexander out, couldn't I?

Alexander put his gun away and climbed into the front seat beside me. Taking my hand in his he placed a worn piece of paper in my hand.

"See, here is his birth certificate. My aunt, Paula, is listed as his mom. You remember meeting my Aunt Paula, don't you?"

"Actually, I do remember Paula. She's been dead now, for what ten years? There's no way, I can confirm your story. Just say for your purposes that I believe you. Even if you and Jack are cousins, that doesn't prove your other claims."

"Natalia, look at me. Jack had some guys kidnap me and take me to Mexico. He dumped me in some drug lord's territory hoping they'd kill me. Instead, thrown into a jail cell, accused of murder and drug trafficking, I plotted my escape."

"But they found a body. They said the corpse was yours."

"Jack said he'd found a body double. He said you think I was dead."

"You've were there for five years?"

"They held me in a fake name and I escaped. I came to rescue you."

"Rescue me? What about our kids? If Jack is really so dangerous why would you leave them with him?"

"I didn't. A friend picked them up at the school and took them to a safe location. Don't worry Ivana and Gregor are safe."

"A friend?"

"A woman I know, Caroline Hensel."

I admit I almost fell for the story then, but I knew Caroline too. She had always been a rival for Alexander's affections. What were the two of them up to?

"Take me to my children, and then disappear again with this ludicrous story."

"Natalia, you have to believe me. If I ever meant anything to you..."

"What do you expect me to do? Believe you instantly?"

Alexander reached over pulled me close to him and pressed his lips tightly to mine. My lips tingled and my whole body felt like it came alive. I felt his hands start to roam, in that moment I knew what I had been missing, craving his touch. What can I say I was weak, putty in his hands. I started to believe Alexander and remembered how he'd always made me feel like I was the only one in the world. I lost myself in the kiss that seemed to go on forever. Then we heard a knock at the steamed up windows.

"Is this her?" the man asked.

"Yes," Alexander asked.

"Come on then, leave the car and let's go. I had a hell of a time finding you Alex."

"I'm not going anywhere," I cried suddenly afraid of this new man.

"I think you are," the man answered pulling a gun and gesturing for me to get into his car.

"Hey don't hurt her," Alexander cried.

"But before you get in put these on," the man placing plastic cuffs on us both.

"Alexander," I whispered, afraid "Who is this?"

"Trouble," he answered.

"Manuel this isn't necessary, I would have come to you. Honest."

"Do I look like a fool Alex?"
"I never took you for one. I'm grateful..."

"Are you? You'd never know it. Where's my money?"

"Money? What's he talking about Alexander?"

"Don't pretend you don't know what I'm talking about, Alex? You said she was bueno for the money. So, why doesn't she know a thing about it?"

"I wasn't talking about her, but you know that. You should let her go. I'll take you to your money."

"I watched the way you looked at her. She might not be the one you said you could get the money from, but she can get me what I want."

"How's that?" Alexander asked.

"Because first I'm going to have some fun and then I'll torture her if you don't give me what I want."

I admit it. I shook to my bones when he said this. This man, Manuel, with his slick-backed long hair, tied in a ponytail scared me. His eyes were dark, so dark that light barely lit them and the smile he shared made one petrified not at ease. Once more he had the bodyweight to back all of this up. He must have weighed two hundred and fifty pounds most of this muscle. I felt the need to get us out of this quickly and safely. We'd cooperate, at least I would.

"I can get you some money. No need to harm me or dicker with him," I exclaimed.

"You can get me two hundred thousand dollars?" Manuel demanded incredulously.

"Yes, it might take a day or so, but I can get the money."

"You have that kind of money Natalia?" Alexander asked.

"I'll empty my retirement savings plan and give it to him, provided of course he'll let us go."

"You give me the money and you two walk," Manuel agreed.

"Ow! What was that for? I probably have a black eye now, Manuel. Wasn't the kick you gave me, before I got in the car, good enough? I'm probably lame from that kick alone."

"Just a wake-up call for you Alex, remember I always follow through."

"What is the money for?" I hazarded to ask trying to diffuse the tension.

"I helped that bastard escape and he promised me two thousand dólares only he no cumplió,"

"No cumplió con? I'm sorry I don't speak Spanish," I explained.

"He says I failed to honor the deal. But Manuel you didn't give me time to get to Caroline."

"This Caroline cares about you enough to give you two thousand dólares?"

"Yes," Alexander exclaimed tersely.

"But you've been to Caroline's. So where are my dólares?"

"I told you I'd give you the money. You don't need to deal with Caroline. She hates him anyway. She wouldn't give him the money."

"Then it's up to you then Natalia." Manuel answered,
"What bank? And do not cross me. I have seen the children
at this Caroline's. They are yours; are they not Alexander?"

"Actually they are Natalia's."

"Do not lie to me, Alexander. They are both of yours.

The boy is the spit image of you. The girl looks like
Natalia. So let's us how you say prescindir de las bromas?"

"He wants to dispense with the pleasantries."

"He is pleasant?" I whispered.

"Hush Natalia," Alexander, whispered back.

"You should listen to your man. I am most pleasant when I
am given the chance. Now which bank?"

"The Bank of Montreal."

"Remember no, funny stuff. Go in the bank get the
paperwork going and then come out. Got it?"

"I've got it, just don't harm my children."

I entered the bank and waited in line. The bank was packed,
odd for a weekday, I thought. The line had about ten people
in and I was number ten. The line inched closer. Three
people were now in front of me when I heard, "This is a
stick up. Everyone down on the floor! Hands on your head!
No fast moves, and no alarms! Do it now."

The robber wore a leather coat, and wore a black hoodie pulled up over his head. He brandished a machine gun in his hands. I wondered how he was able to obtain one in Canada. But I guessed all things were possible, when it came to crime. I just wished he had picked another bank to rob.

It was then that I heard the sirens and knew that when I came out of the bank... if I lived, Alexander and Manuel would be gone. I didn't know where Caroline lived. Could I find my children and protect them? And could I bare to lose Alexander again, if Manuel retaliated?

I glanced at the robber. He looked to be older, perhaps sixty years old, with gray hair to his collar and gray sideburns. He had a low gravel-like voice. He argued, and then demanded they hurry up and give him the money, but something about seemed familiar. He licked his lips and his mustache moved, like it was a prop. I tried to place the voice, but I couldn't. I squinted at him, but his face was totally unfamiliar. I glanced around, and realized that everyone around me was on the floor. Should I be too?

The robber had started shouting and I hadn't heard. What had he said?

"Lady, I said put this coat over your face and put your hands behind you."

He wanted me to put a coat over my face. Why, I didn't know, but he had the gun, so I obeyed. He grabbed my hands, twisted them behind my back and tied them with some kind of material.

"Come on move it. I have the money and we're going."

"We?"

"Yes, we...hurry the cops will be here soon and I for one don't want to be arrested."

"Why do you take me?" I dared to ask.

"I need a hostage, just till I get away," he said loudly, like he wanted others to hear.

We ran, or rather I was pulled out the door, and behind the store next door, away from view. The robber took off the coat off my head. He then picked up a duffle bag there and without warning, yanked at the hair on his head. With surprise, I realized he wore a wig and a face mask. He wasn't an old man at all. It was someone I knew well. He took a knife and snipped off my wrist restraints.

"Jeffery? Is that you?"
"Hello, Natalia. Long time, no see."

"You robbed a bank?"
"I thought Alex was dead and now I find out he is alive. Of course, I did. My brother needed some money to pay that Federale for breaking him out of prison."

"Federale?"

"Yes, that man, Manuel, with Alex."

"If he doesn't get half a mill, he threatened to kill Alex."

"But I offered him two hundred thousand from my retirement savings."

"He probably thought he'd get back both."

"You ruined it all. Why did you take me?"

"I need a hostage, just till I get away," he said loudly, like he wanted others to hear.

"Alex said you'd be there and to grab you for your own safety. Come on we have to get in the van now."

Alex knew that Manuel would capture us? He knew we'd go to my bank? Was I that predictable? I'd had enough I pulled away to go home.

"I'm not going anywhere," I insisted.

"Yes, you are, Natalia. I still have the gun and your hands are tied and I promised my brother. Besides look...," Jeffrey countered.

Jeffery opened the side door of the van, and pushed me inside. I glanced back and in the third seat, sleeping peacefully, were my children, Ivana and Gregor. In the front driver's seat, I saw Caroline Hensel.
"Ivana? Gregor?" I spoke softly.

"They won't answer. You might as well save your breath," Caroline responded, pulling the van into traffic.

"What did you do to them Caroline?"

"Though they have the misfortune to have you for their mother, I love their father, so I didn't hurt a hair on their heads. I gave them some cold medicine and it knocked them right out."

"Cold medicine? They're too young for cold medicine."

"They're still breathing. Quit your bellyaching."

I wanted to say something to Caroline, but Jeffery reached out cautioning me not to so.

"Where do we go?" I asked, instead.

"We meet Manuel.

"But what about Alex?"

"Manuel said he'd let Alex go if we handed over the money," Jeffery answered.

"Don't get any ideas though, Alex is mine," Caroline commented.

"You said you were over him," Jeffery whined.

"Really Caroline? Alexander is still legally my husband."

"You're married to two people. What is the word for that? Oh yes, bigamy. Isn't that a crime?" Caroline quipped ignoring Jeff.

"I didn't know Alexander was alive," I protested still being cautious. I didn't want to make her angry while she drove the van.

"So you married his cousin?" Jeffery admonished.

"You thought he was dead too, Jeff."

"Yes, but if someone I loved died, I wouldn't have married two months later," Jeffery commented.

"You wouldn't be pregnant with twins, alone, broke and scared either."

"Oh whine, whine, whine, it's never your fault is it Natalia?" Caroline exclaimed, banging the steering wheel.

"Watch the road, Caroline. I'd like to get to my brother in one piece."

"We're almost there. There the warehouse."

"I'm not getting out of the vehicle. You two could be walking into a trap and someone has to protect my kids."

I said standing my ground,

"Fine, Alex would never forgive me if anything happened to his kids but I'm taking the van keys."

I watched as Caroline and Jeffery walked over to the decrepit warehouse. Jeffery gun in hand entered first.

Seconds later I heard loud bangs from a gun. Just when I wondered if I should pick up my kids and run Jeffery came out holding up an injured Alexander. He placed Alexander beside me and climbed into the driver's seat.

Seconds later Caroline climbed into the front passenger seat. It was then we heard the police sirens and Jeffery gunned the engine. I only hoped we could escape the police and get Alexander to a doctor as his side had a hole in it from a bullet wound.

A car followed us closely pulling up beside us I saw a gun raised at us and worried they'd hit the children.

Bullets zinged the van.

"Shoot them Caroline," Alexander commanded.

"Hang on, I've got better ideas," Jeffery claimed.

Jeffery gunned the van's engine and started turning down random streets in a serpentine fashion. Seconds later we had somehow lost the car following us.

"Who was that?" I asked but no one answered.

"Why is Natalia here? Natalia was supposed to be left in the bank," Alexander complained.

Somehow when I heard this instead of being relieved, I was hurt that he planned to leave me behind.

"What? Caroline said you told her that Natalia and the kids had to come," Jeffery exclaimed.

"My children are here? Why do you cause me such grief? What have you done Caroline? Why didn't you leave the kids with your mother?"

"My mother is blind in one eye and deaf. The kids are better off here."

"Sure, my children drugged and travelling with bank robbers and thugs and police chasing us is all wonderful," I commented irate.

"Shut up Natalia, they're alive. Now you being alive, now that could be changed," Caroline snarled.

"Caroline!" Alexander barked.

"I know she's the mother of your children. She cannot be replaced blah, blah, blah."

"Caroline, I love you as soon as she gives me a divorce darling we'll be together," Alexander soothed her.

I wondered why he appeased Caroline. Was she behind his problems? At that moment I hated her.

"See? What did I tell you Natalia? He loves me."

If I hadn't felt Alexander's hand in mine signaling to me that he told Caroline a lie; sign language telling me that he loved me, I would have been devastated by this statement. I wanted to bask in the fact I had his love, instead I put on an act frowning and seeming sad.

Caroline seemed happier and calmer after that. She probably would have had Jeffery stop the car, if we hadn't seen a police car. Trying to look nonchalant, Jeffery drove normally as the police car followed.

Finally after a half an hour, we lost the police car as he turned off and Jeffery turned into a residential neighbourhood; where we seemed to turn around in circles. Alexander pale and sweating worried me. His side didn't seem to be seeping blood anymore, but it should be looked at there was a lot of blood on the seat beneath me from him.

"I hope you're headed to a doctor for Alexander," I stated.

"Alexander is hurt?" Caroline asked.

"You didn't notice when he got in? You're not very observant are you? You really love him. Don't you!!."

"Shut up you stupid biotch. I wasn't the one who married his enemy," Caroline responded.

"Good grief Caroline, can it. Are you okay, Alexander?" Jeffery asked.

"I've got a small hole in my side. I think it's just a surface wound," Alexander answered.

"We will go to my old boyfriend Callum. He owes me. He's a vet he can fix you up no questions asked," Caroline offered.

"Are you sure? I don't want him calling the cops, just because he's jealous."

"Yes I'm sure, besides Cal's moved on with Saul, my brother. Go to five hundred and sixty Thorold Avenue," Caroline answered.

"Fine then!" Jeffery answered, turning the wheel and the van towards the street that would take us there. Taking a breath he then asked, "How did this happen anyway Alexander?"

"Manuel's 'friends' arrived. They wanted some cash needless to say we didn't have any. I ducked Manuel didn't."

"So he's dead?"

"Yes, he's dead, but his compadres also want me dead."

"What will you do?" I asked.

"Try to make a deal," Alexander answered.

"We're here," Jeffery announced.

"Let me go first and smooth it over with Cal."

I watched from the van as Caroline rang the bell and a man looking like a linebacker answered the door. He shook his head at her and his stance said he was angry. Then he stared at the van, frowned and motioned 'come on' with his hand.

Jeffery came to help Alexander out of the van and I noticed a pool of blood beside me next to Alexander. Distracted by the children starting to wake up, I looked over at them.

"Mommy? Where are we?" asked Ivana "I have to pee," Gregor complained.

"I'm hungry," Ivana chimed in.

"Bring them in Natalia. They'll be safe. I promise," Alexander begged.
I didn't want to remain in the van and the children both needed something to eat. Maybe this Cal would feed them? I had to get my children out of this situation. I climbed out of the van and felt blood drip down my leg.

Odd, I didn't realize how much Alexander had bled on me. I thought the blood was under me. I stepped out and my leg buckled under me it was then I realized I'd been shot. My head started swimming and I felt faint. I struggled to remain upright as the kids clamoured out the other side of the van. The ground came up to meet me and I knew no more.

I awoke in a dark room not sure of my surroundings. I remembered being carried into a room and having a man put a mask over my face and I now had an intravenous line in my hand.

"Natalia?" a voice asked sitting in a chair near the bed.

"Who are you?" I asked.

"My name is Callum. Do you remember being shot?" Callum asked softly.

"No, but I remember bleeding then fainting."

"You had a lot of blood loss. Alexander told me that he and Jeffery were the same blood type as you, so I transfused you with some of theirs. The bullet wound should have been superficial but it nicked a blood vessel. I repaired that. I've given you antibiotics. I also stitched up that no good Alexander. His wound took three stitches. I wish he had endured more pain."

"Where are my children?"

"Ivana and Gregor sleep. They were really distressed worrying about you, but after they saw that you were sleeping and Saul fed them they relaxed. Saul was able to take them into the backyard and played football with them. Then he took them to the park at the end of the street where they played on all the equipment. Ivana loved the swings and Gregor loved the monkey bars. Caroline went with them. Trust me they're sleeping peacefully; they're fine."

"Tell Saul, thank you."

"You can tell him yourself. But what about you, are you a prisoner?"

I didn't answer. Was I a prisoner? Alexander and Jeffery had held a gun on me. They'd also kept my children from me. Why did I feel any loyalty to Alexander? Did I really feel affection for him simply because I once loved and lost him? I had been shot at and so had my innocent children. I, who'd never been in trouble even once in my life, had now been involved in a bank robbery. I had fallen into the same pattern I had once been in, falling Alexander explicitly, trusting his every word. He had men chasing him! How did I know that anything Alexander, or his cohorts, had told me was the truth? Why did I cling to him? Did I want our mutual destruction?

No, it was lust pure and simple. I had to be stronger than that, if only for my children. Jack had been a good husband and father to me and my children. I only had Alexander's word that Jack had betrayed him. I thought back to our courtship, mine and Alexander's. He had lied frequently, so why did I trusting him now? I had fallen into a romantic fantasy of mine from the past where Alexander would come back from the dead and bring romance and love. Simply because marriage was hard work and I felt neglected.

What had Alexander really brought me? Nothing but fear, pain, and now misery! I had to get myself together and escape with my children. My children had to come first. Callum had helped by patching me up, but could I trust him? He was Caroline's ex.

"I saw the restraint marks. I know someone restrained you," Callum continued.

"It was the man who took me and Alexander. When Jeffery robbed the bank and Manuel took me prisoner. Manuel restrained me," I explained, carefully gauging him.

"Jeffery robbed a bank? Is that how both you and Alexander were shot?"

"No, that was Alexander's pursuers."

"I can help you and your children escape from them," Callum insisted.

"But I thought you were Caroline's ex."

"I am, and her brother is my husband, Saul. But neither I, nor Saul, would want you, or the children harmed."

"Alexander kidnapped me from my car," I admitted.

"I thought as much. Alexander Romanov is a user. He used Caroline. She seemed over him, when she had the misfortune to date me. I was in denial of who I am and thought that she could be the woman to change me.

Instead I hurt her, terribly when I fell in love with her brother."

"Is that why she said you owed her?"
"Yes, she hasn't spoken to me, or Saul, in six years."

"But if you help me she might not speak to you ever again."

"Caroline needs to get away from him too. Saul and hope she'll see him for who he truly is, if you and the children aren't around. Besides Saul and I, couldn't live with ourselves if anything happened to those kids."

"Caroline loves him you'll have a hard time getting her to leave him."

"Maybe, but we have to try. First we have to help you and the children get away. Is there someone I could call?"

I wondered if I should I call Jack? Jack would come and help me and the children get away, but wouldn't I endanger him? I must have looked flummoxed, because the next thing I knew Callum said, "It's okay I know you're worried for the children's safety. We'll make a plan and help you escape over the next few days. In the meantime, mums the word."

I watched and waited for Callum to leave the room. I listened as I heard a door close down the hall. Now was my chance, I'd find my children and we'd leave. I couldn't trust any of these people; despite what Callum had said. I had to get away without any of them knowing. I opened the bedroom door being careful to not let out a sound. I crept into the hall treading carefully as to not make a sound. I darted to the left listening for the sounds of my children sleeping. Ivana always made a soft gurgling sound when she slept and I was sure that is how I would find her and her brother. I opened a bedroom door to see Alexander sleeping; apparently he made the same noises as his daughter when he slept. I closed it carefully so he wouldn't awaken. I then continued down the hall searching for the children.

"Where do you go Natalia?" Caroline asked "I'm looking for the bathroom," I answered.

"Likely story. What do you take me for? An idiot? I know you were looking for your children, so you could escape."

"Caroline, don't you think it would be easier for you if my children and I were out of your hair and Alexander's?

"As if Alexander would allow that."

"He doesn't have to know. Help me and you'll never have to see us again."

"He'd never forgive me," Caroline complained.

"I told you he doesn't have to know help me escape and plead ignorance. Without me and the children you can have all of Alexander's attention and if you have your own children with him, he'll be entirely yours."

"It would be nice not to have your sniveling brats around soaking up all Alexander's attention," Caroline admitted.

"Fine then, I'll give you some money. You can take a cab to the Tim Horton's on Wellington Road and call Jack. But you can't tell him where we are. Even if you hate me and I know you do... you should appreciate that Saul saved your life. If you tell anyone where we are Saul could be arrested. You don't want that do you?"

"I don't want any of you arrested. "I lied, "I just want my children and I to go home to my husband."

"Fine, then start walking there's a phone booth on the corner, they haven't removed yet, call a cab there. Here's the change for it and here's twenty dollars that should pay for the cab," Caroline said taking money out of her purse.

"Thank you Caroline."

"Just go, before I change my mind. The children are in this room," Caroline indicated a room close by. "I'm going back to bed now, so I can deny I knew you were escaping."

I woke the children and told them softly to not make a sound and that I would buy them a donut when we got to Tim Horton's. The children dressed quickly out of the men's tee shirts they had been sleeping in and back into their clothes. I set the tee shirts aside, they smelled putrid I hoped the children didn't. As we crept down the hall I heard a noise and worried that we'd be caught. We snuck out the front door and I shut it softly. The children were excited and started to chatter about the donuts they wanted.

"Are you okay now mommy? Are we going home to Daddy Jack, now?" Ivana asked, while Gregor just sucked his thumb. Funny, how when he worried he always craved his thumb.

"Yes, we're going home to Daddy."

Gregor smiled then and took his thumb out of his mouth.

"See I told you," Ivana commented.

I reached the phone booth and told the children we'd take a ride in the cab to the donut store. They were excited. I waited for the cab and when it came I climbed into the backseat relieved. It was then I heard the locks click in place and realized I couldn't get out. This might look like a cab; but this wasn't one.

"Hello, Mrs. Alexander Camden," the driver stated, waving a gun at me.

"Who are you?" I asked, with fear still trying to exit the car.

"Someone who wants to meet you and your children," he answered, sinisterly.

"You leave my children out of this," I answered.

"But Alexander did not. He owes me money."

"How much? I'll gladly get you the money. Just let me and the children go," I pleaded.

"That would be satisfactory except for one thing."

"What's that?" I asked.

"I also want Alexander. Now dial call him now."

"I don't know his number," I admitted.

"Don't lie to me."

"I'm not."

"Then take me to him you know where he is correct?"

"I do, but do you promise not to harm him or anyone else there?"

"You aren't in any position to bargain lady," the man insisted.

I frowned at him and held my ground.

"Fine, I promise not to kill Alexander. Provided he can pay me back every penny he owes me with interest," he qualified.

"Can I drop off my children first?"

"What do I look like a taxi? The address now!"

"Can I drop them at school?" I pleaded.

"Fine, then you tell me where to find Alexander."

He drove to the nursery school where I dropped off the children and asked the nursery school to call Jack to come get them in an hour. I lied and said they had a doctor's appointment.

"The children are safe, you on the other hand are not, Mrs. Camden, now give me the address before I reconsider my kind impulse and get the children back."

"Five hundred and sixty Thorold Avenue," I answered, shuddering, but resolved my children had to come first.

I went to the door Carlos' gun in my side, his two men following, the other waiting in the car. Opening the door I entered to find Caroline.

"Why are you back here Natalia? Penitent?" she asked, then seeing Carlos and his men behind me, she blanched, then asked, "Carlos? Why are you here?"

"My darling Caroline, are you not pleased to see me?"

"I thought..."

"You thought you never see me again. You believed you could run away with Alexander?"

"I didn't run away with Alexander. He has a wife and children," Caroline said softly, in a voice I'd never heard her use.

"I forgive you chiquita. But you need to come home."

"I can't Carlos."

"You are mine. You will obey me," Carlos answered striking her face.

"You don't own me, Carlos," Caroline whimpered.

Carlos and Caroline were interrupted by Saul and Callum who walked down the hall arm in arm. Carlos stared with revulsion at the two of them.

"Who are the fresas?"Carlos asked.

"Why does he calling them strawberries?" I asked.

"Oh grow up Natalia, and shut your mouth. He insulted my brother with a derogatory term."

Appalled I wanted to say something, but then I remembered the slap and to my shame I was silent. Callum and Saul continued to hug like Carlos didn't exist, but I knew they heard and I smiled.

"One of the mayates is your brother. It's a sin against God."

Disgusted once again with Carlos, I frowned at him. He didn't notice, all his focus centred on Caroline.

"He can't help who he is. It's how he was born," Caroline answered.

"Nonsense, it describes such a perversion in the bible as a sin against God. I should kill them where they stand," Carlos cried pointing his gun at them.

"Please, Carlos. Saul is family, Carlos. He and his friend do not harm you. Please do this as a tribute to me, a token of your love," Caroline simpered, placing her arms around Carlos and hugging him. He let go of me as Caroline then kissed him full on the lip.

"For you dulzura, I will allow him to live and his amigo.

But you will owe me," Carlos insisted.

Carlos then pulled Caroline closer to him and held her fast to his side.

"Who is this Caroline?" Callum asked.

"Do not acknowledge him Caroline," Saul retorted.

"So the skinny one is your hermano?" Carlos asked "Yes," Caroline answered.

"No one must know that he is your hermano. What is the English word? Brother?"

"You'll leave them alone?"

"As long as you come with me."

"You will not go back to him. He beat you so bad, I thought you would die," Saul cried pulling Caroline, behind himself and Callum.

I had some empathy for Caroline then, the poor woman had been abused and now her nightmare had found her.

"Do not interfere little hermano. Your sister wants to see her son again. Don't you caricias?" Carlos asked an evil grin on his face.

"Luis is dead," Caroline retorted with tears lingering in her eyes.

"Who told you such a lie?" Carlos asked an evil gleam in his eye as he took out his phone and playing a video.

Caroline's eyes grew big as she watched the video of a little boy kicking a soccer ball and she advanced to touched the screen in awe.

"My baby...," she cried.

"See our son will rival Pelé."

"But Javier said...,"

"Did you tell my wife our son died, Javier?"

"Only when you told me to boss," Javier answered.

"Shut-up Javier," the other bodyguard quipped.

"So see you have much to come home to our son needs his mother; but first I must speak with Alexander. Where does the basura hide?"

"He went to the store to get milk," Saul answered.

"Then we'll wait for him, won't we Javier and Marco?" Carlos exclaimed

"Yes, boss," Marco answered.

I listened to all of this with amazement and fear. Carlos the criminal, had not only married Caroline, but had a child. Poor Caroline, she needed to get away from him. I needed to escape and save us all. I could go through the bathroom window I decided

"I have to go the bathroom," I retorted.

"Go, before I change my mind," Carlos commanded.

I went past Saul and Callum to go to the bathroom and Callum pressed a piece of paper in my hand, without Carlos noticing. I shut the bathroom door and opened my hand and read the note. It said...,

The RCMP are on the way. Hold tight. Alexander and Jeffery are locked up and safe in the basement.

After a few minutes, I flushed the toilet and ran the water. Just as I finished, I heard a crash as the front door broke open. Shots rang out and I jumped in to the bathtub, hoping I would survive the gun battle.

The sound of bullets seemed to go on forever, hearing a break I stood up still worried about the destruction of the bathroom door from bullets. In the process of going through the window, my legs in the air, squeezing through the small window. I wiggled out the window and dropped to the ground. I heard bullets begin to whiz again. As I looked back in; one bullet came through the bathroom door and split the tub I'd been sheltering in. I ran, hands raised, straight to the sidewalk; where I saw men in flak jackets that read R.C.M.P.

A lanky good looking man stepped out of the shadows and pulled me into his arms.

"Thank God, you're safe Natalia," Jack exclaimed and then kissed me passionately.

I wondered at that moment, why I had entertained and thoughts of Alexander in any romantic sense. Jack loved me, all of me. He had come to save me.

"Where is that bastard Alexander?"

"According to a note, Callum, passed me, Alexander and Jeffery are locked in the basement. A man named Carlos holds Caroline, Callum, and Saul prisoner. He took the kids and me prisoner but I got him to drop the children at school..."

"They are safe with my mother Natalia. You did good, honey."

"How did you find me? Did the police call you?"

"No..."

"It's all over Mrs. Camden. Carlos Ramirez is dead. Did you get her statement Jack? Does she know where Alexander Camden is?" an R.C.M.P. officer asked, interrupting.

"She says that Alexander and his brother Jeffery are locked up in the basement, and the other two, Bob?" Jack asked

"His body guards Javier Rivera, and Marco Batista have all been arrested, as well as one Manuel something. Javier is in serious condition the paramedics tell me, but they think he'll make it. The other one has a few flesh wounds. Paulo Georgiou was apprehended before we started all this, you know that Jack."

"Carlos' second?"

"There was a raid in Mexico, César Montez got away."

"Damn!"

"You know what this means Jack. Do you want to tell your wife or am I?" "What aren't you telling me Jack? Is it that Alexander and I are still legally married?

Alexander told me that. Alexander said you put him in prison in Mexico...that you knew he was alive. That's not true...right?"

"I didn't put him in prison. I heard he was died. Then I heard about you and at first I wanted to just help you out, after all he was my cousin. But then I fell in love with you. I wanted to take care of you and have you take care of me."

"But you knew he was in prison at some point?" I asked, reading between the lines.

"I admit, I found out before we married that C.S.I.S. found him alive, in some Mexican prison. They got him to sign the papers you're legally divorced and therefore we're legally married. The guy I talked to lied to me about Alexander. I swear I didn't know about him being alive. They told me he was dead more than a week before got married. I only found out when you went missing. They contacted me and told me Alexander was alive and had taken you. I gave them an ultimatum if they wanted my help, they had to start sharing."

"How do you know anyone at the Canadian Security Intelligence Service? Or the R.C.M.P.?"

"I'm sorry Natalia, I lied... I've been lying to you about my work. I work for the R.C.M.P., we do some work with C.S.I.S. I used to work mostly in the office not in the field, in cyber terrorism mostly, but then my cousin became a person of interest in a lot of different crimes and they brought me in to help track him. Surprised, they trusted me I started to track him. I found him in Mexico and then I lost him until they found him in a jail. I thought they totally trusted me, until a few months ago, when they finally told me Alexander was still alive,"

"You worked for the police? But you said you worked in an office for TriCorp. You went on business trips, or so I thought. All those times you were working for the R.C.M.P, in danger and you never told me?"

"I couldn't they told me I was sworn to the official secrets act."

"But you're telling me now."

"I know, I told them that I could lie to you any longer. That keeping secrets had almost got you killed. I'm sorry Natalia, please forgive me."

"I was the one originally involved with Alexander. You weren't responsible for him taking me but you should have confided in me, I'm your wife."

"I should have, official secrets vow, or not," admitted Jack.

"But you love me?" I asked. "So why have you been trying to push me away for the last few months with all those comments about my weight gain?"

"I love you, Natalia, but when I learned Alexander was alive and you could be a target for him and his cohorts I tried to get to leave me and take the children."

"But you weren't always mean to me..."

"I tried but I loved you too much I couldn't let you go."

"You're a dope you know that," I commented "But I love you. Can we just go home to the children?"

"I'd like that, but the truth is, Bob went to pick up our children and my mom We're going into the witness protection program, after you give your official statement at the police station. César Montez will come after anyone who is Alexander's family."

"Then Alexander and Jeffery will be in danger."

"I love that you care, but Jeffery and Alexander will be going to jail and will be protected there. Caroline Hensel, her son (whom we rescued in Mexico) and her brother Saul and Callum will be relocated into witness protection too,"

"I'm glad they're safe. But will your Mom be okay with this?

"Mom wants to be with her grandchildren and us. She is anxious to go start a new life."

"Where will we live?"

"I'm not sure they haven't enlightened me. But wherever it is I'll be happy with you."

Six months and one week ago, I as Natalia, to all intents and purposes disappeared. We live in an idyllic small rural area in British Columbia. Our house is far from other people and the children take the school bus into town to go to school. We get together for events with the neighbours but mostly we keep to ourselves.

Jack still gets reports from the R.C.M.P, but they are addressed to Jason Hendrickson. He works as a game warden and keeps the peace and stays close to home. My name and the children's names have changed too. I'm Nancy Hendrickson and my children are Ingrid and Geoffery. The children thrive they love the outdoors and have adapted well to their new names. My mother in law seems happy living with us in the wilderness, something that surprised me. We've learn to bake bread and bonded over the children. As for me and Jack or Jason as I call him, we're better than ever, because we now tell each other everything. In fact I have a surprise for Jason in six months, another child we'll join our family, and I for one can hardly wait.

~0~

Max Justice

I raced up my office stairs, anxious to get a little of the

hair of the dog. I had wrapped up the Collins' case last night and I admit I did a little more celebrating than I'd normally do. Mr. Collins had been so happy with the return of his gem, that he kept insisting I drink on his dime. I'd try to curtail the amounts; but he kept refilling my glass and now I paid for it. Here it was mid-afternoon the next day and I'd just rolled out of bed. I felt I needed to put in a presence at the office. My head ached like little demons had taken residence, taking turns with little hammers pounding on my temple. My stomach swished like its contents, were ready to become a cascading hot spring as I walked down the street.

As I reached the block where my office was I noted a big black boat at the curb. Had I missed an important client? I hoped not. Flush or not, that dough wouldn't last forever, I could use another case. I picked up my pace and raced up the stairs. To my surprise, I could see my office door busted open. A flatfoot in uniform stood by the door and when he saw me he yelled. What gave? A copper wouldn't be driving the boat I saw at the curb.

"Stop right there."

Someone had broken into my office. I hoped it wasn't the trouble that had brought me here. If they found me I was done for. Being related to both Moran and Capone was not a plus. They had wanted me to choose a side, so I chose me. Relocating to a city neither of them frequented was the hard part; but I prided myself on difficult.

I considered scarping from the copper, but I had done nothing wrong; though I still stood like a deer in the head lights. I needed to calm down and quit looking guilty.

"Thank you Paul. I'll take over the questioning guard the door. Follow me sir," the plain clothes copper demanded.

"Yes, sir," I said following him.

"Sit," he ordered.

He had the nerve to sit boldly in my desk chair and motioned for me to sit at the client chair. I resented his dominance and his use of my property. I kept meaning to fix a loose spring in my chair, now I hoped it would bite him on the ass.

"What has happened here? How may I help you with your enquiries?" I asked putting, on a cultured deep voice I sometimes used for snooty upper crust clients.

"Who are you and what is your business here?" the man demanded.

"This is my office. I am Max Justice."

I looked at the door with dismay. To get the door fixed would take a lot of my hard earned money. I guess I wasn't as flush as I thought. The G-man flipped open a badge and I wondered why he was here on a simple robbery.

"Mr. Justice, where could I have found you between five a.m. and seven this morning?"

"I was at a tea party," I quipped.

"Mr. Justice, these quips will get you nowhere."

"Someone broke into my office and you disturb me with questions?"

"Someone not only broke into your office but they left you a present."

"A present?"

The flatfoot pointed to a spot on the floor. I hadn't noticed until now. A rusty stain on the floor, along with pooling blood said someone had not only been hurt here; but had died here.

"Who?" I asked stunned.

"Do you know a Candance Schwimmer?"

"Who?

"You may have known her by her working name Candy Cane."

"Will Candy be okay?" I asked gulping.

I'd last seen her three months ago. Candy had some hard luck. Her male relatives had abused her so she run away to the big city and had joined the oldest profession. Now I found out her last name was Schwimmer. Just what I needed, she was related to one of Capone's lieutenants. At least I was alive. She was not poor girl!

I'd tried to help the dolly out. I found her a job as a shop girl; but the owner had found out her former profession and had try to blackmail her. Candy had run away back into her old life. I tried to get her to leave again, but she told me she didn't want to see me anymore and her pimp kept me away. Now she was dead; was it my fault. Should I have worked at it harder? Blood of the innocent put inside my office as what... a warning or payback? Maybe it was time to move on. Time to find a new place to open shop.

"No, she's dead. You seem all broke up. Mr. Justice," he snarked.

Anger threatened to boil to the surface at this remark, but I controlled my thoughts and let it pass. Breathe in, breathe out, without being too obvious. Rule number one? Never show anger to a copper, or in this case a G-man.

"Do you know why anyone would kill the girl in your office?"

"No, sir, I don't. I hope you catch the killer. Can you tell me how you found her?"

"Keep it up boyo. Politeness will get you nowhere! You're not fooling me."

"My grandmother taught me to respect authority, sir. I am a law abiding citizen," I answered, "Now please sir, how did you find her here?"

"We'll play it your way for now then Justice. We received a call from your next door neighbor. They said they thought you were having a wild party. When the uniforms arrived your front door was broken and Miss Schwimmer lay dead in a pool of blood. As if you didn't know!" The G-man explained.

"I liked Candy, and I wasn't here. I was working a case," I stated.

"Likely story, Justice. I'll be checking your complete alibi. For now give me your address."

"One hundred, twenty-five, Penny Lane, I have a room there," I explained.

I was eager not to have the man look too closely at me; though I legally changed my last name I didn't want any connection to my old life.

"You better not be holding out on me Justice. I've met your kind before you're nothing, but a two penny private dick. Don't even think about sticking your nose into this. We don't need your kind mixed any more than it is, in my inquiry. While our investigation continues your office is off limits too for the next two days,; so don't be getting any bright ideas or you'll be getting a taste of the hoosegow."

"Can I least get a man in to fix my door? Someone's liable to walk off with my stuff?"

"As long as he stays out of the office and only replaces your door and you don't..."

"I know don't leave town," I answered.

I didn't like that a G-Man had been called into this. I could only see trouble ahead. Maybe I should just scarper out of town while the going was good? No, that would make the cops look at me even closer. I had to wait this out. They find the goon who snuffed Candy and then I'd get my life and office back. It couldn't have anything to do with me. I hadn't ticked off anyone in at least a week. I pulled up the cover on my overcoat walked out of the building and walked over to the new place, Abelson's around the corner. At the counter I sat down and flirted with Kelly the waitress. Kelly brought me enough coffee to steady my nerves and a bagel to settle my stomach and I was grateful enough to leave a big tip but not to big I had to fix my office after all.

I headed out to an appointment with my client, Giorgio Palmano at Club Newberry. Searching behind me and seeing no one I still gave any followers a merry chase as I led them through back alleys and behind buildings all over town. Finally when I believed it safe, I arrived at the backdoor of Club Newberry. I wrapped the secret knock and was admitted.

Escorted to the table by a pretty waitress in a tight little number, I found Giorgio sitting and drinking Cuban coffee. Handsome and very Latin looking despite his Italian roots, Giorgio's black hair gleamed and shone under the lights as it curled at his collar. His eyes black as coal looked at me with genuine friendliness as he gestured for me to sit down.

"Thank-you Selena," Giorgio stated.

"You're welcome Giorgio, I mean Mr. Palmano," Selena all but cooed.

I raised an eyebrow and Giorgio smiled at me and winked.

"That will be all Selena," he said as she lingered.

I'd known Giorgio in my other life and owed him a favor. He had wanted me to find his sister Gina. This was the follow-up meeting to address my findings. I'd found her, but I doubted Giorgio would be happy to know where. She was a dolly to a mobster, Louis 'Little New York' Campagna. She sang in his club and warmed Louis'bed. How do you tell her brother that?

Not to mention I had avoided Louis like the plague; hoping he wouldn't penetrate my disguise. But any further contact with Gina and this case might bring me more into his sphere. Why did I want to avoid Louis 'Little New York' Campagna? I hadn't crossed him if that's what you're thinking. Louis 'Little New York' Campagna and some of the other mobsters he associated with thought my dead father had hid money from Capone and that I alone knew where it was.

"Maxie, how good to see you," Giorgio quipped.

"Please Giorgio, lower your voice and call me Max."

"Do you really think you're fooling anyone with this short hair and that fake nose? Let me help."

"Giorgio, I am not a delinquent or hapless. I told you..."

"I know...that you hide in plain sight. People believe what they see. The men must be blind in this town not to see you're a beautiful woman, Maximilliana."

"Giorgio..."

"Marry me Maxie. One word from you and I'll take you away from all of this. I can protect you from your Uncle Frank and your distant cousin Bugs."

"Giorgio, keep your voice down one word and ..."

"Fine, I'll not reveal your secret, Max. I won't pull the trigger and no need to get all worked up. Did you find Gina?" he asked whispering

"Yes but don't shoot the messenger. Gina's with Louis 'Little New York' Campagna."

"She isn't! She can't be!!"

"She is, I'm so sorry Giorgio."

"Not for long if I have a say and I do. You might not see me for a while Maxie, but I'll be back. Thanks for finding my sister. Here you've earned this. Keep safe," he said peeling off some bills.

I wondered if I should follow but then decided he was a big boy, Giorgio could handle himself. I left and went to my residence. Imagine my surprise when I got out of the cab to find coppers at my rooming house and a hole where my room used to be.

This was getting tedious I thought. Tedious? Who was I kidding? I was lucky to be alive. Who could be behind this and why? Standing behind a tree across the street; so I'm not seen, I watch the fireman sift through my belongings and prayed they wouldn't find my other breast binder and realize what it was. Then I realized I was about to blow my wig and that would reveal my cover faster than you could say Jack Robinson. All my carefully made suits were gone; so much for being flush, no work place, no home, and no clothes. I took a moment to wallow then pulled myself together after all things had been worse. I had some cash in my pocket I could afford to have a new suit or two made. Then I'd find a flop house to hunker down until this all blew over.

Why had someone blown up my room? Were they on to me, or was this work related? Could my work with Candace have caused this? She was after all a Schwimmer. Some private dick I was. I hadn't even ferreted that out. Did someone assign my demise, or was this just a warning?

I heard a sound behind me and pivoting on my foot. I wound my foot around my opponent's feet and took him down placing my foot in his chest. Deep laughter came from his chest.

"Hush," I countered.

"Cara mia, do you want to do the Rhumba? I could offer you a place to stay. I think you could find the dance very tempting."

"Giorgio, how did you find me?"

"Maxie, I've known where you live for a while, but when I heard your office had been blown sky high I worried and followed you, for your own protection. I don't want to see you in a Chicago overcoat."

"As you can see I need no protection."

"Maxie be sensible. Some trigger man has targeted you.
You need my help Maxie. Please let me help I could take
you to my home. You'll be able to come and go as you
please with no interruptions and no strings."

"Really? No strings like waking up with you in my
bedroom at night?"

"Maxie, you insult my chivalry. The only way you'll find
me in your bedroom is if I'm invited," Giorgio claimed,
looking at me with those velvety brown bedroom eyes.
I considered the costs and the safety. It was possible that
some hatchet men had targeted me. I'd be safer at Giorgio's
he had plenty of his own Bruno. He was a man of his word
as much as he'd like to be in my bed he'd never press me.
Plus I had to rebuild my office door and then get my office
professionally cleaned to remove the blood on the floor.
Then I had to replace all my clothing or at least get a suit or
two. My money would not go that far if I also had to pay
for lodging besides a flophouse held the dregs of society
and they often wandered in your room at will, I reasoned. If
I picked up a lock at the hardware store and the tools I
could install a lock at Giorgio's and get my food and
lodging free. It could be a win-win situation for a while.
It wasn't like I'd stay there forever and become his ball and
chain or his doxy. I found myself nodding.

"Snazzy. Now quit bumping your gums and scooch into my
limo. Carl will drive us home."

"Max Justice? So we meet again and who is this with you?"
the G-Man asked creeping up on us.

"I'm just leaving with my friend who offered me a room for the night since your investigation has triggered my room's disappearance."

"You insinuate that my men did this? How dare you?"

"Now G-man; pull up your shorts, that's not what Max said," protested Giorgio.

"So that's how it is? This is your boyfriend, Max?"

"How dare you? Listen up good, egg. Just because you have a buzzer doesn't give you the right to insult my pally. I'm dizzy for his sister, Carmen. Surely you've seen Carmen Palmano, the canary at Club Newbury?"

"That clipjoint? Carmen wouldn't give the looks of you the time of day."

"I'll have you know I run a respectable joint," Giorgio protested.

"Carmen has been seen with many men; but never you, Max Justice. Carmen's blinkers only see the egg man and I hear her lamps are focused solely on the wet smack who owns the joint, Passion Pit owned by one Louis 'Little New York' Campagna."

"My sister doesn't have eyes in her head. She wouldn't know a dead hoofer from a crumb bum but even she wouldn't get mixed up with the likes of Louis."
"It's true then? Carmen is hanging around with that greaseball?" the G-man fired, narrowing his eyes and putting his laser focus on Giorgio he then continued, "So you're Giorgio Palmano, Carmen's brother?"

"I am, Giorgio Palmano and Max is one of my best friends. Now what will you do to find the people who done this to my pally?"

"We're looking into it but you should pick better pals." The G-man responded to Giorgio, then turning to me he said, "Where did you go after you left your office this morning?"

"I met my friend Giorgio for coffee at his club. Was anyone hurt?"

"Your landlady is dead. You got her killed. She was outside your room when the bomb went off."

"Helena Gierga is dead?"

"Yup, what's left of her has been identified," the G-man countered.

"What the hell? I got her killed? Helena Gierga was a good decent woman and something in your investigation got her snuffed. I want your name now!!" I exclaimed.

"Why Max I didn't know you cared. My name is Detective Ellis Jamie. I work for the Prohibition Bureau of the F.B.I."

"The what?" I asked.

"Part of the FBI that looks into organized crime role in operating under prohibition."

"Then what brings you here? You should be in the big Apple, or Chicago."

"Funny you should mention Chicago. I just got word a few minutes ago that a hit went down at a garage. Peter and Frank Gusenberg, Albert Weinshank, Adam Heyer, James Clark, John May, and Dr. Reinhardt Schwimmer were all shot. Some Valentine's Day they all had. All of them dead, but Frank and he aint talking! Cops asked who shot him and he said no one; but he's lying in a hospital bed expected not to live. Now maybe you better cut the pretense and be straight with me boyo, because it looks like you're on their Valentine's list."

"That had nothing to do with me I don't know those guys. I keep my nose clean and do some sleuthing. I don't hang out with the mob," I protested.

"Who said they were the mob?"

"Everyone knows the mob hangs out in Chicago and who else would sanction a hit? Don't insult my intelligence."

"How about you Palmano?"

"Why aren't you out finding out who killed Max's landlady, instead of quizzing Max? Or doing your real job and finding the hooch that people are smuggling into this city? And that's Mr. Palmano to you. I am a business man with a club and I obey the law," Giorgio griped.

"That's not what I heard Mr. Palmano. I heard you had bathtub gin for the right price and some Cadillac."

"How dare you? You trumped up house dick. I serve coffee, liquor is prohibited. You're whacky."

"A little hot under the collar, Palmano?"

"I'll not be made you're patsy. Go and find someone else to bother."

"Bother? It's no bother. Just remember wet back I have my eye on you."

"I think we'll be taking our leave now. I'm sure if you have any more news of the people who have threatened me you will contact me at Giorgio's won't you Detective Jaime?" I asked.

"You betcha!" Detective Jaime responded belligerently, "Oh and one other thing... don't leave town grease balls, I might have some more questions for you."

I swept up from the table putting on my male act, my daddy's signature walk all bravado and swagger that I'd seen every day of my life. Giorgi followed me making it a point to flirt with the waitress on the way out. We got into Giorgio's limo which was at the curb and Frank drove us away. Peering in the side view mirror I watched the G-man enter his car and follow us. Frank lost him at Fifth Street and I laughed.

"I hate that copper," Giorgio claimed his eyes blazing with anger.

"Don't blow your wig, Giorgio. Usually you're so cool what set you off?"

"Those were my friends killed at that garage and he just rattled off their names like they was garbage. That two-bit blowhard, pill!!"

"No tell me what you really think about him," I exclaimed and then I asked, "Who do you think was behind that hit?"

"Probably Capone in conjunction with some Chicago cops his got them in his back pocket."

"But why would Capone send some boys after me?"

"He wouldn't. I don't think these two things are connected. You'll have to let me put out some feelers Maxie and get the skinny on what's going down here."

"I don't know Giorgio; you could get hurt," I whispered in his ear not trusting the driver Frank.

"Maxie," he whispered back "I won't let anyone find out your secret. You can count on me."

What could I do? I left this in Giorgio's hands for now; but once I found out who did this I would use Giorgio's contacts and make them pay for giving my landlady the kiss off. Helena had been a sweetheart, the real deal. She gave me a home and had waited for the rent a time or two when dough was scarce. I'd make them pay with their lives. I vowed. I looked up I needed to make a stop before I arrived at Giorgio's and lucky for me it was up at the next block.

"Giorgio, get Frank to stop at the next corner."

"No time for stops. We're headed home; before the G-man catches up," Giorgio complained.

"I need to go to my tailor," I complained, "And I have an appointment this afternoon with a client."

"Maybe you should take a vacation. Someone could be sending you a message with that body showing up at your office and your room getting toasted."

"It's easy money, a cheating dame and a husband who just wants to dump her."

"This is how you make your money?"

"It's a living Giorgio."

"I apologise, of course you have to being home the suds," Giorgio responded, then turning to his driver he commanded, "Frank take Max to his tailor."

"Where do we go Max?" Frank asked.

"Drive to Monsieur Bordereau's on 8th street. It's on the next block, 801."

"That derelict building? My tailor would be more suitable. Frank drive there," Giorgio insisted.

"No he wouldn't."

"Fine. Frank to Monsieur Bordereau's on 8th street."

"Yes, sir," Frank replied, looking back at us I could tell Frank wanted to hear more of our talk and I didn't like it. I trusted no one but Giorgio.

"You could be living in the lap of luxury if you'd followed through, doll face," Giorgio suddenly said.

"The walls have ears Giorgio," I cautioned.

"I admit to surprise when I heard you'd spirited yourself out the window and left Tony high and dry," whispered Giorgio.

"Someone conveniently blew up a car in the parking lot and I was able to escape while they were all distracted," I explained with a lurch of my eyebrow.

"Okay, so I admit it. I knew they were forcing your hand and to hitch you to a fat crumb bum, old man like Tony the Tuna...while not if I could help it."

"You were the one that left the envelope with a thousand dollars in my purse too?" I whispered back.

"Yah...I did and I slipped some medication in Tony's coffee too, just enough to make him sick. They took him to the doc right after you bolted."

"I'm grateful; I'll pay you back one day Giorgio. I promise."

"Just stay safe Max."

"We are here sir," Frank announced.

"See you later, Giorgio.

"We'll be back in an hour to escort you to your meeting."

"I don't need a babysitter Giorgio," I complained.

"No you need a keeper, or perhaps a friend and I'm your friend Max."

"I know you are and thanks again, Giorgio."

"One hour, see ya."

I stepped out of the car and stared at the store it was decrepit, but the work, the artist of the tailor, Monsieur Bordereau created was sublime. I entered the store watching as Frank and Giorgio drove away. Monsieur Bordereau personally greeted me.

"Remercier le bon Dieu tu es vivant,"

"English, Monsieur Bordereau."

"Sorry, I've just been so worried, thank the good lord you are alive."

"You heard about the explosion?

"Oui. You lost all the suits I made you?"

"Yes."

"Bon, then I will make you new ones I have your measurements on file. You haven't gained any weight since then have you? Maybe I should take new measurements. Now come with me and try on this suit, ma petite. If it doesn't fit then I will take new measurements."

I followed him then looking back to make sure no one could hear us, I asked, "Grand-père Bordereau, can't it be just the two of us now?"

"Yes, darling girl. Andre and Paul are busy out the front, they can't hear us now. What's going on ma petite, Maximilliana? You are être bien embarrassé."

"Yes, it's a bit of fix; but it will shake itself out. Don't worry!" I answered.

"Je savais être un gumshoe ne serait pas sûr. Do you need some money to leave town?"

"Being a gumshoe is a good occupation a really good cover for me. I don't know if I'll need any salad grand-père, I'm flush at the moment; but I do know that between Giorgio Palmano and I will get to the bottom of it. I'm not leaving town. They can't make me!"

"That's what I'm afraid of I didn't save you from that awful marriage just to have you wind up dead and involved with Giorgio Palmano."

"I'm not involved and I'm not going to get killed," I protested.

"We'll see. I love you ma petite fille. You are the best of my petits enfants.

"Je t'aime aussi, grand-père."

"Your French accent is atrocious, but I would protect you with my life."

"I'll be okay. Giorgio will keep me safe."

"He had better. Try the suit on fille chérie. I'll wait here."

I tried on the suit in the dressing room, setting my gun and holder on the bench. I finished and glanced in the mirror. I looked pretty good, it would pass as Max. I was startled to hear the front door open and Andre's and Paul (Grand-père Bordereau's assistants) murmured greetings; then the rapid sound of gunfire. I grabbed my gun off the bench and dove to the floor. I pulled grandpère into the dressing room and we stood on the bench quietly waiting for them to leave. Grand-père wiped away tears and pulled me towards the backdoor of the shop. Hearing footsteps coming closer, I hid behind a dress dummy and grand-père behind a table. Two men with machine guns looked around moving benches and the curtain to the dressing room. One of them went back into the front while the other continued to look. I held my breath as he came closer to grand-père's hiding place.

The shooter's back to me I pulled out my gun and fired through a pin cushion to muffle the sound. The gunman, too quick on the draw, fired back at me striking me in the shoulder. So much for my replacement suit, I thought then caught myself this was a life and death situation and I worried about a suit? I grabbed grand-père with my other arm and we ran out the backdoor to more shooting from the gunman.

Was this some superman? I hit him full on the chest he should be falling down instead he'd struck me again. A bullet grazed my ear and the side of my head. Grandpère pulled me towards the curb just as Frank pulled up with Giorgio. The gunman was hot my heels as Giorgio yanked us in the car.

"You're bleeding Maxie," Grand-père insisted.

"It's a flesh wound," I commented.

"Maxie, that's an awful lot of blood pooling on my suit.

"Sorry, Grand-père."

"This old geezer is your great grandfather?" whispered Giorgio, "Wait a minute did he say blood, Maxie..."

"Yes, to both, but don't let Frank hear you," I answered.

"Maxie we have to get you to a sawbones."

"I'm fine, truly fine."

"Quit lying," Giorgio stated.

I felt faint but I resisted it. Finally when I felt I could resist it no more I stated, "I'm just going to close my eyes now."

I felt hands on my jacket removing it then pressure on my wound then I passed out.

~0~

I awoke disoriented and confused. Then I remembered the dead girl, the bombing and the shooting at Grandpère's. Dressed in a silk nightgown I blushed wondering who had clothed me.

"Wonderful, you're awake, Maximilliana," the woman said coming into the room.

She was tall with long black hair. If you didn't look closely at the small wrinkles beside her eyes and mouth you might think she was in her forties; but somehow I thought she was at least fifty.

"Who are you and how do you know my name?

"Maximilliana, don't you remember me?"

"No, should I?"

"I'm Giorgio's mom. You came to my house when you were a child. What have you got my boy into now? My Giorgio has been in love with you since he was a boy when are you goin' make him an honest man and me a grandmother?"

I looked at her surprised, how could I have forgotten Giorgio's mother? Her eyes black and sharp and her hair colour black as coal, were the duplicate of Giorgio's; that alone should have told me who she was.

"Mrs. Palmano, I'm so sorry..."

"Maxie, call me Sophie, and I'll forgive all of this if you'd marry the big lug and make me some grandbabies," she pressed again, "Maxie, my boy adores you don't look so surprised. Right now he's chomping at the bit outside your door just waitin' for me to tell him he can come in. Now how do you feel?"

"I'm a little sore in my shoulder and my leg," I answered, "But how is grand-père and Giorgio?"

"As I said Giorgio's just worried about you. Your family awaits outside."

"Family? My grand-père?"

"Your mother and he are outside."

My mother? My stomach began to hurt and I felt like I'd throw up. Mother would be so angry because I ran away. Why had Giorgio allowed his mother to call my mother? I had to get away. I swung my leg over and tried to stand up and would have fallen flat on my face if Sophie hadn't caught me.

"Stubborn just like my boy. I can see why he likes you, Maxie. You always were feisty. Now stay in that bed cover yourself up and make yourself presentable while I get my boy and your family."

Mom came in followed by Grand-père. Mom's hair now had hints of gray funneling through her dark brown hair. Her eyes the colour of black jade stared beadily at me. Mom looked scared and sad at the same time and I felt guilty.

"Maximilliana, how dare you scare me like this? I didn't know where you were and I thought you were dead...that they had killed you." My mother gulped through tears.

"Mom, I'm sorry."

"I'm just glad mon père took you in and looked after you after that fiasco of a wedding. Your uncle should never have made such a deal with Anthony Giacomo. I'm so sorry baby. I should have stood up to him. I shouldn't have allowed it to get so far that you had to run away."

"It's okay, mom."

"It's not okay. You told me you didn't want to marry Anthony that day. I slipped some money into your purse; but didn't help you escape and now Tony may have found you and Grand-père...,"disassembled my mother openly sobbing.

"Mom, it's all going to be okay."

"Cher, let's not quibble, our girl is better," Grand-père answered.

"Can I join this reunion?" Giorgio asked from the door.

"Come in Giorgio."

"Is it Tony? Has he really targeted me?" I asked.

"It's not Tony and I don't think the target was Maxie," Giorgio answered.

"Who was the target then?"

"I'm sorry Maxie, I'm the target. You were just collateral damage."

"But you've never done anything wrong. You have no mob ties."

"It's my fault," Sophia claimed, "I should have told you sooner, Giorgio."

"Told him what?"

"Who my dad really was," Giorgio answered.

"Who is your father?"

"He's a lieutenant for Jack "Legs" Diamond."

"Maybe I should take my daughter and flee," mother cried.

"I don't think that would work now, daughter. They've targeted people near and dear to Giorgio, and Maxie is very dear," grand-père explained.

"Explain this to us, how could you get involved with a thug?" I asked.

"How did you?" Sophia asked.

"Touche, please go ahead and tell your story."

"I got involved with Paulo Garbino before I knew who he was and then I found out I expected Giorgio. I ran away and Samuel Palmano took Giorgio as his son and raised him so until he died two years ago. Dutch Shultz found out recently. Somehow he recognized me after all these years. He counted back and then he figured out the truth that Giorgio was Paulo's son. He's gone berserk. I think he's gunning for Giorgio to get back at Legs, since his father works for Legs," Sophie explained.

"What can we do?"

"I'm going to find a way to keep him off my back once and for all," cried Giorgio. "And here's the plan Frank helped me come up with. We retaliate against Gus Shultz. I'm going to hire some guys going to start by attacking some of his businesses and whack some of his men."

"Are you and Frank fatheads, or just sauced? You think you're going to dust off Shultz's businesses and men and he just going to roll over and say he'll leave us alone? This is habitual. You act like none of the women near you have a brain," I griped.

"She's right son and that's a stupid plan. He'll never leave us alone; especially if you retaliate. All we end up doing is making him mad," Sophie cried.

"I'll not be a part of this and neither will my daughter and granddaughter," exclaimed grand-père.

"Innocent people get killed that way Giorgio," my mother cried.

"If he doesn't leave us alone will clip him."

"Do you hear yourself Giorgio? You sound like your Daddy. I didn't leave Chicago and raise you with Samuel so you could be a gangster. I wanted better for my boy."

"I'm trying to save our lives, mother," Giorgio complained pulling out guns out of cabinet in the room.

"I know son, but as Maxie told you this isn't the way. God all mighty that's an awful lot of guns you own. You can't use them this way Giorgio. You just can't!!"

"Then what do you suggest we do mother? Pretend it's not happening?

"How do you know it's Shultz? Wasn't Candace related to one of the Schwimmer's?" I asked.

"Yes, but Shultz knew you were my friend Maxie and he targeted you and your client to get back at me and my father."

"You're sure boy?" Grand-père demanded.

"Listen to him Giorgio," Sophie urged.

"Really mother? Do want me to have a new father figure? Paulo Garbino is my father and you kept me from him. I'll just go listen to him."

"You think it was that easy? That I wanted to know to get your father to leave me alone? I didn't know he was married. I was a good catholic girl sheltered and innocent. One night in his embrace and you were conceived. When I went to tell him the skinny, ball and chain gave him an ultimatum. Get rid of the dolly (me) or she'd leave him. He chose her," Sophie cried, sounding dejected.

"You almost sound sad mother, I thought you told me he was a crumb bum."

"He was...he is," Sophia answered.

"Bickering and recriminations get you nowhere. I ought to know. Do you know how my wife died?" Grand-père interjected.

"She died from the influenza," I answered.

"It's time you know Maxie and Marianna knew what happened to her. Maria became depressed after your birth, Marianna and she needed something else other than being a mother. She begged me to take her to some clubs and get out of the house. I didn't understand and I tried to discourage it. I thought she should spend all her time with you, Marianna. She went anyway without me. She met some people who offered her a job as a canary six nights a week. She loved it and she booze it up with them as well."

"Sounds like a bad business," Giorgio commented.

"Maria liked to hoof it and party with the men that came into the club. I tried to reason with her."

"You busted her chops?"

"You wouldn't have hit her Grand-père?"

"Busted her chops is scolding, Maxie."

"Oh, sorry."

"She wouldn't listen. I divorced her and got custody of you Marianna. I let her see you regularly, but one night the club was burnt to the ground. My Maria died," grandpère choked his voice heavy with unshed tears.

"I'm sorry about your wife Mr. Bordereau, but what has that fire to do with this?"

"It was one of Shultz first jobs. He burnt the club down. I tried to kill him with some French Canadian pea soup; but the bastard didn't eat it. It seems he doesn't like ham. He still doesn't know that I tried to poison him."

"You tried to kill him? You who wouldn't harm a fly?" I demanded, incredulously.

"Any man can be pushed to far. It took years of planning and willpower, but I seized my chance. The soup incident happened just before I moved here."

"You could have been killed grand-père," I insisted.

"I know but I had to try. It was just before his friend; Joey Noey was whacked in front of the Chateau Madrid last year. I know Shultz ordered the hit on Arnold Rothstein shortly after. That's why I stopped trying I couldn't risk retaliation against my family. Shultz won't quit until he whacks us as well. We should flee while we still can," Grand-père answered.

"He'll just follow us," Sophia complained, "What can we do?"

"Something drastic," I stated.

"I don't understand Maxie," grand-père complained.

"Something none of us are will like; but especially you, Giorgio."

"Tell me what you're thinking Maxie," Giorgio demanded.

"We get all our money out of the bank and all our valuables together. Then we let them see us go into your club while we leave by the back door and it explodes."

"You want me to blow up my club?"

"Yes."

"But where would we go Maxie?"

"We'll flee to Canada. You still have some cousins there don't you grand-père?"

"Oui."

"Is that a yes, or no, Mr. Bordereau?" Giorgio asked.

"Yes, I have cousins in la belle province."

"Huh, la belle province?" Giorgio uttered.

"He speaks of Quebec. It's the beautiful province," I explained.

"Close enough,"grand-pere said.

"I don't speak French and neither do my mother and sisters. So how can we flee there?" Giorgio demanded.

"Don't you have cousins in Ontario, grand-père?"

"Oui, some cousins in Stratford, Ontario.

"Can we get in touch with them and ask them to find us some birth certificates?" I asked.

"Certificates?"

"Yes, we get the cousins to scour the cemetery, perhaps in nearby London. It's a bigger city after all and they should be able to get some names and ages close to ours from the cemetery."

"I don't understand Maxie," my mother complained.

"We get their names and we become Canadian citizens and hide in plain sight. That's dynamite, Maxie," Giorgio commented.

"We'll have to learn their language. Don't they say eh a lot and speak with English accents?" Sophie asked.

"Mother, they speak English like we do; maybe some of retained a little of their English ancestry in their accents; but not all of them sound like that. Their slang is a little different, but we'll pick it up in no time."

"What if the girls, your sisters won't go. Giorgio?" grand-pere asked.

"My sisters will do as I say and save their lives. This might take a couple of weeks though so you all have to act normal and go on with your lives with some thugs by your sides to keep you safe. As for Maxie she can continue to recover here," Giorgio answered.

"Don't I get a say?" I asked.

"No the doctor wouldn't want you moved. He said you needed rest after your ordeal," my mother declared.

"Ordeal, mother? I have a bullet wound in the shoulder and leg. I'm fine."

"Fine? We almost lost you with that infection. The doctor says you're on the mend now but ....," Mother then dabbed her eyes.

"Nonsense! Don't exaggerate."

"You've been out of your head with fever for two weeks Maximilliana."

"I haven't! It can't have been two weeks," I cried.

I then tried to stand up then remembering my sheer nightgown I wrapped the blanket around me. Of course my leg gave out and Giorgio caught me.

"Now this is also why I'm staying," my mother declared, "No billing and cooing on my watch."

"Mother..."

"That's right I am your mother and I'll protect your virtue."

"Oh...." I cried exasperated, "Let's get started with this plan."

"The only thing you'll do is rest. I'll make sure we're set," Giorgio exclaimed.

"I can do my part."

"Please Maxie, just rest and get better."

A knock was heard at the door and the door opened. "You have visitors, sir." Clive, Giorgio's butler said as he came in the room.

"Who is here, Clive?" Giorgio asked.

"No need to stand on ceremony, Clive. I'll just speak to your master. Ooh, have I missed a party."

"You are a very rude flatfoot," my mother cried.

"He's not just any flatfoot Mrs. Justice he's a G-man. His name is Detective Ellis Jamie. He works for the Prohibition Bureau of the F.B.I," Giorgio answered.

"Really if you are such a sophisticated copper, Detective Ellis, than why do you barge into my daughter's bedroom?"

"As I said I thought this is where the party was. You and your brother look a lot alike," Detective Ellis commented.

My heart in my mouth, I had visions of Detective Ellis identifying me as Max.

"That is because they're twins." My mother quickly answered.

"Can you tell me where your son Max is, Mrs. Justice?"

"I think he went out of town, after I yelled at him, because his sister was injured."

"You were injured Miss Justice?"
"Someone shot at Max and missed hitting me. I'm told," I replied in a very high pitched soft feminine voice.

"Those two guys we found at the tailor shop. They were your brother's bodyguards?"

"I told you, I don't remember the shooting," I whined. I fluttered my eyes and looked fragile trying to fool Detective Ellis.

"You don't remember? Yah, you seem all distraught that two men lost their lives," Detective Ellis said sarcastically.

"Detective Ellis, they were my employees. I am Monsieur Boudreau. Miss Justice came to my shop with her brother to wait while I fitted him for a suit I told the officers this at the police station. I called for help but as I told the officers I fled with Miss Justice to protect her. I now visit her."

"I find that odd. Why would you come to visit Miss Justice? Do you know Miss Justice well?"

"No, but I feel responsible she got hurt at my shop."

"I also find it convenient that she does not recall the shooting."

"How dare you? My daughter has been very sick for nearly two weeks. The doctor believes the memory loss is probably a side effect of her illness possibly to protect her from the horror."

"So none of you know where I can find Max Justice?"

"No, "Giorgio answered, "But why do you want him?"

"Someone destroyed Mr. Justice's office again and we found another body we're trying to identify. Do you have any information about his Mr. Palmano?"

"I don't know anything about this and neither does the Justice family. You're barking up the wrong tree. Maybe you should be ferreting out the real culprits and quit bothering decent folks like us and a sick woman," Giorgio replied squinting his eyes in a menacing manner.

"Giorgio...,"I cautioned grabbing his arm.

"Decent? You people don't know the meaning of the word." Detective Ellis laughed, and then turning to me he apologized, "I'm sorry for disturbing you Miss Justice. It was a great pleasure to meet you and your lovely mother. But the two of you should watch the company you keep. Giorgio Palmano has a record and ties to the mob."

"Don't you speak of my son that way you dad-blamed, trumped up copper, with illusions of grandeur," Sophie said,

"Hush mother, he's just trying to get under my skin with his gobbledygook."

"Hint a nerve, Mrs. Palmano?"

"Leave my mother out of your games."

"Gladly, Mr. Palmano, when you start telling me the truth."

"Listen fathead I'm a businessman as I told you before G-man. I run a club and serve Cuban coffee where people have a good time and I know nothing of Mr. Justice's whereabouts.

"Sure and all the illegal booze in this city isn't regulated through your speakeasy, Mr. Palmano."

"My son sells coffee and runs a club where people have a good time drinking that coffee. How dare you? Leave! Now!!"

"My mother's correct. Maybe it's time you leave before I inform your superiors you've been harassing a sick woman."

"I'm leaving because I want to but I'll be back. Mr. Palmano."

When Clive had shown the G-man out the front door and we all heard it close downstairs Sophia commented, "That man will be trouble. I hope he doesn't ruin our plans."

"Me too," I said softly.

A week went by and as I fully recovered I saw a lot of
Giorgio. He brought me candy flowers and friendship.

We spent hours together talking; I almost didn't miss that I
couldn't be out doing private eye work. He also asked me
every day if I would marry him and live my new life with
him in Stratford, Ontario, Canada. I found myself agreeing,
for I'd fallen in love with him and he didn't expect me to
act like the typical housewife. I knew it was irrational, but
with Giorgio, I felt complete and safe. He told me I could
have a career, if I wished when we moved to Stratford. I
was astounded but happy. Giorgio definitely knew the way
to my heart.
He was never sullen and smiled at life so much. I needed
that. He did however put his foot down about me
continuing as a private investigator. I almost gave him back
his ring and dismissed him. Then he explained how we
couldn't have the same careers; or they'd find us so I finally
was force to agree. Giorgio told all of my clients that I the
office was closed and I had disappeared with my
permission. It all seemed unreal, that I could be happy
amongst such lingering disaster, but our plans were made.

Giorgio and I announced our engagement to our mothers,
my grand-père and his sisters. They were all very happy for
us. Our mother's smiled like they had planned the whole
thing. Maybe they did I wouldn't put it past either of them
and neither would Giorgio.

We decided to marry in a simple quiet ceremony in the Catholic Church with just our mothers, his sisters and my grand-père. No one would be notified ahead of time except the priest and then it would be safe for all of us to be in one place at the same time. Grand-père insisted on designing my wedding gown. This delayed our departure as the material came from France. Giorgio seemed happy about this in any case, as he claimed his man had not scouted out Stratford enough. Nor had he gotten all the necessary fake documents, we would need from the forger only the documents for our mothers, his sisters, and grand-père. So time was on our side if we must wait.

The day came for our wedding and I found myself torn. Was I marrying Giorgio because of the fix we were in, or did I truly love him enough for a lifetime? I still headed for the church, deciding I could hoof it like I did the last time.

Arriving at the church and entering the room, that I was to change I still felt to undecided. Was love enough?

My mother sensing my mood smiled and pointed to gaily wrapped gifts in the corner; then she left me for a moment as she went to the water closet.

Any doubts I had were dismissed when I opened the gifts Giorgio left for me in the change room. Giorgio had left a blue sapphire necklace, a small bouquet and a rope ladder for me. The note with it said...,

My dearest, Maxie

The sapphire necklace is your something old and blue. It
was my grandmother's and now it's yours. The flowers, red
roses for my true love, baby's breath for your pure heart, a
purple berry rose, to tell you to choose your destiny, I won't
give up my promise, I'll love you forever, and lastly the
rope ladder should you decide you can't marry me; or just
to remind you, you always have an escape. I hope you
won't use the ladder, but as I said with the berry rose, I'll
love you forever.
Yours,
Giorgio

Giorgio was the one I decided. His love letter was distinct
as he was. He valued my independence and wouldn't
squash it and I loved him. Love would be more than
enough. I marched down the aisle proudly.

The priest began the ceremony and had just reached the
words, "Should anyone object let him speak now or forever
hold his peace," when a man entered the church.

He was tall over six feet and built like a linebacker with his
head down. Frankly I thought he was a goon out to scope
out the place and so did Giorgio. Giorgio threw himself in
front of me.

"Sorry, did I interrupt, Giorgio?"

"Paul is that really you?" Giorgio cried and I relaxed a
little.

"Maximilliana, this is Paul Spano. He was my best friend
when we were kids but I haven't seen him in years,"
Giorgio explained then turning to Paul he asked, "How did
you know about my wedding and where it was?"

Sophie my soon to be mother-in-law blushed.

"Your mother contacted me. She thought you'd like me to be here," Paul explained.

"Mom will talk about this later," Giorgio said to his mother, then turning back to Paul he exclaimed, "I'm glad you came Paul. Please join us afterwards were going to Cafe Dianna next door. We have a lot of catching up to do."

"I'll be glad to. You're a lucky man Giorgio. Your wife, Maximilliana is a beautiful woman. I remember her as a little girl she was pretty then but much more so now."

"Were not married yet," complained Giorgio.

"Oh, now I am sorry," Paul cried sitting down in the first pew beside my mother.

The priest finished the ceremony and we were soon married. Giorgio had rented the café for the evening, so no other customers interrupted when we went next door. Paul and Giorgio spent the rest of the evening talking and whispering in a dark corner of the cafe. Oh okay, so he came over to the table where mother, my mother-in-law and my new sisters were all talking to me a few times, but I felt left out. After all it was my wedding day shouldn't he be at my side? They were old friends and obviously they needed to talk. I would soon have him all to myself; I reasoned, but still I brooded.

As it neared midnight we said our goodbyes and I went home with my new husband to his bedroom. He smiled at me and my heart went pitter-patter and I forgave him. I threw myself in his arms and we made wild passionate love all night. Near dawn, I fell into a deep sleep.

I awoke to raised voices in the outer room and threw on my housecoat over my nakedness. I opened the bedroom door a crack, to hear the G-man raking my husband over the coals. This wouldn't do. We needed to get rid of him, before he found out our plans. Mother, Sophie and Giorgio's sister had gotten a flight to Paris this morning and then would fake their deaths on a return flight and then go onto Stratford without us. The G-man must not find out...could not find out and foil our plans. We needed to lose the G-man fast, but how? How dare the G-man interrupt the most serene atmosphere, I'd had in weeks?

"Thomas Nevel told me that you knew where Max Justice was," Detective Ellis retorted.

"I have no idea where Max is," Giorgio answered, "Thomas Nevel is a liar."

"You expect me to believe that? You two were as thick as thieves, and all my contacts tell me you were the one who closed his office."

I came out of our bedroom and stood beside Giorgio grabbing his hand in mine.

"I have no idea where my brother-in-law is. I only closed the office on behalf of my wife's family," Giorgio answered.

"You're interrupting our honeymoon," I cried throwing my arms around Giorgio and curling my body next to his.

"Miss Justice, do you know where your brother is, or your mother?"

"I have no idea where m no good brother is. As for my mother she's travelling. I think she'll be in Europe any day soon," I answered.

"Likely story, Miss Justice. I demand you tell me where Max Justice is!"

"You are not listening, my name is Mrs. Palmano and I have no idea where Max is. How dare you come here threaten and insult myself and my husband? You've interrupted our honeymoon! Maybe you should leave.

"You wed this knucklehead? What? Do you have cabbage for brains? I can help you get a divorce if you want. Temporary insanity ought to fit the bill," the G-man said touching my arm.

"Get your hands off my wife," Giorgio shouted his eyes blazing.

"Like I said before, I'll take her off your hands any time she wants. Right doll face?" The G-man taunted.

"How dare you? What kind of a lawman are you? Keep your hands off of me."

"You know I'm offering you the deal of a lifetime honey."

"I am not your honey. I am a happily married! I love Giorgio and he is an honest forthright man. Who loves me happens to love me back. As for my mother she has gone to Paris. That's what she told me at our wedding. Mother, unlike you, didn't want to interfere with our wedded bliss. My goon of a brother? I have no idea where Max is. Nor do I care," I answered.

"Right, doll face! Your brother and your husband are upstanding citizens with ties to the mob, so much so that the mob is gunning for them. Do you want to be the next accidental target?"

"My husband and my brother have no ties with organized crime. He ought to sue you for slander."

"I've heard this song and dance before. Just remember doll face if you are involved with this cretin; then you too can anticipate doing the time."

"You leave my wife out of your vendetta against me."

"I'm speaking to your wife not you."

"I think you should leave Detective Ellis," Giorgio insisted, his fists clenching.

"Yes, please leave," I added.

"I'll leave, but you both should remember I'll be watching you, and if I find evidence that you lied to me, or criminal activity you'll both do the time. Count on it," Detective Ellis smiled, his eyes squinting and scaring me.

Then he left out the front door.

"I don't like that man," I said after he left.

"I don't like him either. The way he looked at you or touched you. I wanted to sock him."

"He was trying to rile you Giorgio. What do you mean how he looked at me?"

"He looked at you like you were an ice cream sundae."

"Yuck, I think I'm going to be sick!"

"Now you know how I feel. What's more I think he's a dirty cop; but I haven't been able to prove it, yet. He could be legit, but I do know that he has the hots for you. If anything should happen to me, I want you to go to my safe in the bedroom. Then empty all the money and stocks out of the safe. Take the key to the bus depot lockers, nine through twelve. Go to the lockers and take the suitcases. There are papers and money in one of them; use them and take your new identity and run."

"Not without you."

"Promise me, Maxie,"

"Nothing will happen to you. Will it?"

"No, I don't think so, but I didn't like the way that G-man looked at you. If anything happened to me he could come after you."
"And I'd shoot him."

"I know you would Maxie, but he could shoot at you back. Promise me if anything happens before it's time for us to leave that you'll flee, without looking back."

"But won't that look suspicious won't they look for me?"
"Frank will fake your death and make it look like they got you too. The plane crash with your mother, my mother and sister and your grandfather will occur tonight. Tomorrow we'll go to the club they'll let us know about the plane crash and then the next day we'll fake our deaths."

"Tell me the plan for us again, please Giorgio."

"I'll arrive at the club go about the business of running it. You will arrive as Max, about midnight. You'll smooze until closing time making sure you are seen. Then when everyone has left, you'll go to the basement and pick up the flashlight, I provided. There you'll open the two steel doors with the key I gave you. Walking through the tunnel, you'll arrive at the other two double steel doors. Go through those doors on the other side of the street and enter into the building, I also own. Once there you'll open the other doors, go in the room and change out of your Max disguise. You'll fix your hair to look like Maximilliana and don the dress I placed there.

Waiting ten minutes, you'll go upstairs and exit through the backdoor of the building. Being careful to not be seen, you'll take the back alley to Canter Street. There you will walk down and over to 8th Street and go to the front door of Club Palmano where Frank will let you in."
"Then will all go to the tunnel and make our way back over to the building across the street. Frank has stashed a car on 5th street. We'll take that car to the bus station; grab our stuff and drive to Niagara where we will walk across the border using the papers saying we're Canadian. Our family will be waiting for us in Stratford."

"Sounds like the plan will work. And no one will really be hurt? Where will you get the bodies?"

"My contact dug them up from a cemetery."

"Isn't that risky?"

"No, the bodies will burn beyond recognition as the plane goes down in a forest."

"But I told the G-man that they'd already flown to Europe."

"Their private flight was delayed. Then when they take off it will crash a half- an hour into the flight. The pilots will land drop off our family then takeoff again and parachute out crashing the plane beyond recognition. In the news they'll say just another small plane crashing, with no survivors. As for our doubles? They'll burn in the explosion at Club Palmano. Now promise me, if anything happens to me, you'll flee to Canada on your own."

"Fine, I promise. But you better not let anything happen to you."

"I have one more thing I'd like for you to do Maxie."

"Isn't that enough? I'm supposed to flee without you."

"If anything should happen to me."

"It won't," I protested denying it.

"But if it does, you must act fearlessly. I don't want you to be alone the rest of your life find a good man and be happy."

"I've found a good man and I'm going to be happy in Canada, with you!"

"Of course, my cherry armour. Come back to bed now."

I couldn't help it I giggled, "Did you learn that from Grand-père? I don't think French is easy for you. It's actually my cherie amour, not cherry armour."

"Oh...,"Giorgio stated dejected.

"I'll be your cherry armour any time you want, sweetheart. Now what did you say last night Giorgio, about showing me some new moves this morning?" I asked guiding him back into the bedroom and dropping my robe. He laughed and took me in his arms. It was our honeymoon after all.

~0~

The shrillness of an unanswered phone, constantly ringing drilled into my head. Rising from a deep sleep, I told Giorgio to answer the phone; only to realize, he'd already answered. Giorgio sat on the edge of the bed, his back straight at first and then slumped as the conversation went on. I heard the words plane crash and I relaxed, the plan was in play. He hung up the phone and turned to me; his face ashen and his eyes downcast.

"Maxie...,"he began, but by then I already knew.

"They're dead aren't they? My mom, your mom, your sisters and my grand-père are really dead. You're sure?"

"Yes. Tommy checked into in for me. They boarded a flight to Niagara and the small plane went down with all hands on board."

"No..., Tommy has to be wrong he's mistaken and they're just following the plan."

"I'm sorry, Maxie. I wish to God he was wrong."

"But what happened? How did the plan gone wrong? They weren't supposed to die! It was pretend!!" I wailed.

"The plane took off and about a half an hour into the flight the plane crashed," Giorgio answered trying not to cry, "We don't know why yet but we will."

"They're unto us Giorgio. How could they know of the plans? Who did you share them with?"

Fear gripped me, as I realized we too could die.
"I only told Frank and Tommy and they are loyal to me. They'd die before they'd betray me. It has to be a horrible coincidence."

"Some coincidence, our families have been wiped out."

"I'm devastated too Maxie, don't be disgusted with me because I didn't protect them."

"I know. I don't blame you Giorgio. I'm just so..."

"So wrecked."

"Yes."

"Me, too."

My arms went around my husband. We came together in grief, tears dripping down, being wiped away, then skin against skin, legs entangled, touching, everywhere. Then more tears and embraces. Sometime later, we left our bed and dressed reluctantly. Giorgio got on the phone and made arrangements for our families' interment, as I soundlessly cried. I wiped my tears and steeled myself to remain strong until he could turned to me.

When he got off the phone Giorgio pointed said to me, "Pack what you must keep and we'll leave the rest. Don't pout we'll buy better stuff in Canada."

As if I ever pouted. What did he think I was like every other woman he knew? I reluctantly packed leaving my favourite gun behind. That was the real kicker my gun had to be left behind. I decided to hell with it! I was taking my gun. The G-man didn't know about my gun. I wadded it up in kerchief and stuck it in my purse. It had served me well and there was no way I was leaving my Colt M1911A1 behind. Besides a seven round gun was hard to find. Giorgio actually laughed at this and said of course I had to take my bauble. I finished packing and we went into the living room.

"We can't go ahead tomorrow," I announced, "We have to bury our dead."

"We have to continue with the plan and I'm sorry, but going to the burials is out of the question."

"What?"

"Think about it Maxie, we'd be a really good target at a funeral. Absolutely sitting ducks."

I wiped away tears and tried to think clearly. I knew Giorgio made sense, but the idea of not being there to say goodbye to our loved ones seemed wrong.

"Don't worry. I told no one that plan, except Frank and he's totally on board. It will work," Giorgio reassured me taking me in his arms and wiping away my tears.

"I'm not one to just go boldly with any plan. I'm used to making my own plans and being independent. Are you sure we can trust Frank?"

"Yes. Everything is in play even Anna the maid, has the next two days off. "

A loud knocking on our front door made us fly apart.

"My clue to answer the door," I cried getting up.

Giorgio jumped up as well. Pulling a gun (I didn't know he had) from his waistline, he pushed me behind him; as he pulled open the door standing to one side of it. Giorgio then saw who stood there and slipped the gun into the back of his trousers, before the man saw it.

That damn G-man stood there sputtering the same gibberish, about how I should get away from my husband. He again wanted to know if we had any information to impart that would help him in his investigation of the body found at Max's office and the shooting that took place at the tailor's. Then the man not satisfied with Giorgio's answers, rambled on about how he believed Giorgio's reckoning would come. This went on for nearly a half an hour before he imparted the news about the plane crash. He seemed to take great delight as he wondered around our living room imparting the news, flicking ash from his dangling cigarette into our beautiful crystal vase.

I cried like I had just heard the news and Giorgio comforted me.

The G-man was particularly cruel, as he looked at me with those hawk's eyes and said, "It will only get worse from here. Do you want to die too?"

I stared daggers at him for I just wanted him to go away.

Giorgio became angry on my behalf and looked like he wanted to slug him so I managed a fake swoon. Giorgio carried me to the sofa and then hustled the G-man out of our home with the guise that he had to take care of me. The G-man said he'd be back in a couple of days and I hoped that he meant it; but I still worried that everything we planned would fall apart. For I felt I had allowed myself to be lulled into complacency. Giorgio allayed my fears and we spent our time in bed and honeymooned the rest of the day and night away. Then next morning Giorgio left to go to the club after I kissed him a sweet long goodbye that ended up with us back in bed.

Giorgio had hurry to arrive at the club in time to be seen for the plan would take place today and I found myself torn about continuing, or not continuing. I was to come as Max in the next hour, smooze and then leave through the tunnel returning as myself, but could I? Should I? Nerves, I decided. It was just nerves. I could do this. All would succeed; after all I had Giorgio by my side.

I went to the club dressed in the handsome suit grandpère had made me during my recovery. I hated to leave this suit behind it was so lovingly made, but facts were facts, the corpse must wear it so he could be identified as Max. Near closing time I said my goodbyes and went to the basement to change into my dress to be myself once again. In the basement I dressed the corpse in my suit and then washing my hands I put on my dress. Placing the key to unlock the door and turning the wheel I pulled it open. Putting the key in my purse I had with my dress, I went through closing the door. I exited the other building's back door being careful to not be seen and then I walked over one street. Coming back, I entered the front door and many of the staff greeted me as Maximilliana Palmano, Giorgio's new wife. They wished Giorgio and I, well and seemed happy at our marriage.

Closing the club and watching the staff exit, Giorgio and I waited. Satisfied that only Frank, he and I remained we locked the doors. We went into the basement and Giorgio took my hand.

"Frank will set the charges to go off twenty five minutes from now, that should give us enough time."

I took a big breath and went to go to change out of my dress before Giorgio stopped me crying, "Our rings, we've forgotten about our rings. The corpses need to wear them."

I handed my wedding rings to Giorgio and took off my dress handing that to him as well.

"I'll go with you," I exclaimed.

"No, we need to hurry. Frank and I will go to my office and put them on the corpses along with my suit. But you need to go ahead and wait in the building across the street through the door."

"But...,"

"You'll distract me and the bombs go off in twenty-five minutes. I'll be back in five minutes."

We kissed and I went through the door again. Five minutes later waiting for the door to open again; I was thrown off my feet by a sonic boom.

My head was thrown against the wall, but the door was still intact as well as the walls. I shook my head and tried to think. The bomb had gone off early. Could Giorgio and Frank still be alive? I went through the door and found the building partially collapsed. Going to the office I found Giorgio outside the door along with Frank.
Blood pooled in rivets along the floor. My feet went unbidden to Gorgio's side, refusing to believe at first what I saw. Giorgio was obviously dead. The top of his head was gone. Frank cradled him in his arms and cried over his body.

I stood there in horror, my hand over my mouth, tears dripping silently from my eyes. He could not go to heaven without his wedding ring, I decided. I went into the office and saw the bomb in Giorgio's office still ticking. I glanced at Giorgio's office clock miraculously it still worked.

Fifteen minutes had passed since I last saw Giorgio we had ten minutes to get next door. I then realized that only one, or possibly two of the bombs, had gone off. We must get Giorgio's body into his office and then I must reluctantly leave. I didn't want to I almost decided to die too, but I'd promised Giorgio I'd flee and I couldn't break the promise I'd given him.

With Frank's help, I pulled Giorgio into the office. I took Giorgio's ring off the corpse and put it gently on Giorgio's wedding finger. I kissed his lips and said a fond goodbye.

"Frank, the bomb hasn't gone off," I cried pointing to the still ticking bomb.

Frank grabbed my hand pulled me through the office door, the fake Giorgio corpse on his back. I ran as fast as my legs could carry me. When we heard voices, Frank pulled us to a stop just before we went through the basement door. He threw out the body down the corridor and then we hid behind some rubble, crouched on all fours.

"I thought you said the entire building would come down? Wait a minute who is this? "

"The building will and I think that that's one of Giorgio's bodyguards the other voice said.

"Maybe we should get outside? I've no desire to die."

"Good idea, let's go. That bastard Giorgio Palmano and Max Justice actually thought they could keep easygoing John Scalise from his dolly Gina."

They thought John Scalise easygoing? Were they crazy? And all of this was about Gina? That stupid little twit. She'd gotten my Giorgio killed. I wanted to kill her with my own two hands for not staying away from John Scalise; but then I remembered she was Giorgio's sister. He loved her so like or lump it she was my family now. I needed to save her from herself.

"The boss and his friends Albert Anselmi, and Joseph Giunta grabbed her from a flight that was headed to an airport for Paris. Then he blew up the flight those people that were helping her were on."

Wait a minute, I recognized one of those voices, but I had to be wrong. It couldn't be!!

"Where is Gina now?"

"She's in a downtown hotel with the boss."

No, I wasn't wrong and he would pay for his treachery.

That's all we heard before the two went through the front door of the club. We had five minutes left to get out of this building. We went into the basement and through the door. A minute later we felt the rumble of the explosion and the horrific roar of walls coming down. Like a huge earthquake under our feet, the building seemed to sway, but where we stood there was no damage. Giorgio's safeguards had saved us.

"Did you recognize either of those voices?" asked Frank, "I didn't."

"Yes, I did recognize one of them, but I didn't think this one was bent."

"It was a copper?"

"Not only a copper. He told Giorgio and I that he was a G-man. This bears looking into some more before I act."

"What's his name? He's the first one on my list."

"Not just your list, it's my list too."

"But you're a woman," Frank protested, "You'll cry and keep me from completing the task."

"You know I'm more than that Frank, you met me as Max. I don't whine and cry. I have a level head and they killed my husband."

"Yes, you do have a level head, Mrs. P. and I knew that Max was you, but only because Giorgio told me."

"Then you also know, I have to avenge my husband's death and save his sister."

"You're sure that this is the route you want to go? Giorgio wanted you safe in Canada and I promised him I would get you there if he couldn't."

"Yes," I answered.

"Then I'm in. We'll make em pay, together."

"Thank you, Frank. Now do you know a discreet tailor?"

"I do. Let's go Mrs. P."

Anger burned bright in me in the days that followed. I wanted my husband's killers to pay. We'd taken two rooms in town, under assumed names I was now Xavier Sword and Frank was Richard Gunner. I had disguised myself with a red wig and some more prosthetics from a theater store. I thought I looked ugly and grotesque; but that's what I wanted. I limped now thanks to the explosion so that added to my disguise.

I scoured the city ferreting out information about the two men I had heard before the final explosion. I had hoped they would have been killed, but to my dismay they survived and now I needed to be the one to end their lives, but not before they too had fear in their hearts.

They were staying at a downtown hotel until our bodies were identified and autopsied. Luckily for Frank and I, and unlucky for them, Giorgio's plan had worked the bodies would be identified as ours. Simply because of the jewellery and other identifying marks they had for us.

I watched them unobtrusively from my hiding spot in their hotel lobby pretending to be a bellboy trying to decipher the best way to get them. I needed to make Detective Ellis and my so called husband's friend, Paul Spano pay. No wonder he hadn't seen Paul since childhood it was a set up pure and simple. The man had attended our wedding with smiles and congratulations and then had planned our demise with the G-man.

"Max," whispered Frank.

"Richard," I stressed whispering, "Do you speak to me?"

"Yes, Xavier. It's your break time," Frank covered speaking softly.

"Let's go outside for few minutes."

I hustled Frank out of the hotel lobby being careful that we weren't seen. Then we had our conversations nonchalantly in an alley away from prying eyes and ears.

"What could be so urgent you had to interrupt me when I watched the assholes that murdered my husband?"

Frank blanched at my language but recovered quickly, "I found out that G-man's lying."

"What a surprise. What did he lie about now? Does he have another plan to blow something up?"

"He lied about his name."

"His name isn't Detective Ellis? I should have known.

"Who is he? I want to torture him in his real name."

"Torture?"

"Yes, torture. He tortured Giorgio with fear and intimidation. He gave my sister-in-law to a mobster to abuse, just because she was stupid enough to think him earthy and cute. He then killed my husband and my family. They will pay!"

"His name is Detective Campagna. He's related to Louis 'Little New York' some kind of cousin, I think."

"Louis does have Gina again?"

"No, he passed her onto one of his cronies, Georgy Burke before you rescued her. The man claims he owns her, now."

"Owns? How dare he? I'll show him who owns whom.

Now tell me is he in cahoots with Freddy Burke?

"Freddy Burke?"

"Freddy Burke, a lieutenant of Capone's and his cousin."

"I'm not sure, but if he is we've got trouble," Frank answered.

"More trouble than people trying to blow us up?"

"Yah, maybe we should just go to Canada and let them knock off each other."

"They killed my husband and family and they keep my sister-in-law against her will. I'm not going to scamper off to Canada and let them win."

"Fine, I'll help you Mrs. Palmano. Giorgio Palmano was a great friend and boss. He always tried to keep his family safe. I promised Giorgio that if anything happened to him I'd keep you safe and get you to Canada, but I know he'd want us to save his sister, Gina. The only way to save her is to put the kibosh on those two and the man who sent them after Giorgio. We need to make another mobster a patsy. Maybe make it look like one of those against Capone dropped them?"

"Great thinking, Frank. I know their movements, now I'll we have to do is get them all together, rescue Gina and kill them all."

"Quite the list boss, we've got some thinking to do."

"We'll do it."
"I have no doubt, boss. If I were that G-man I'd be shivering in my boots."

I stood in a copse of trees concealing myself behind them, but still overlooking the fresh dug graves where my beloved husband and the body that had been identified as me, were being buried. My mother-in law and the rest of my family were also being interned nearby. The rain pelted down, a steady drizzle, which seemed to echo my mood.

I wanted revenge plain and simple. Their heads on a platter would be a good start; but I had to be patient while the seeds were sowed for my payback. Just killing them was too good for them. They need to suffer. Frank agreed and had proposed some of the plan that might work but he left half way through the service to ferret out some information that would assist us in getting our revenge.

I noticed with surprise that Paulo Garbino was in attendance. He laid roses on his son's open grave and wiped away tears. Jack "Legs" Diamond stood beside him and I heard Legs loud whisper, "We'll get them Paulo. They'll pay for this outrage."

I vowed then and there, that I would get them first and they'd know it was me; before they died. Before I knew the graveside ceremonies were over and everyone got in their cars. Frank reappeared telling me that he had some news. We too went to my car parked a couple of blocks away across the cemetery.

Frank seemed upset and I wondered why until he started speaking, "Boss I made a mistake. Georgy Burke had Gina, but she's moved on to John Scalise. At least I think she's with John. That's what he is boasting. Georgy and John still talk and do business together and they hatched the bombing plot. They wanted to get rid of any objection to Gina staying with Johnny boy, but word on the street is that she has another guy on the string; though I haven't found out whom!"

"Of course that's what we heard just before the building imploded. Maybe we can save Gina, before they kill her; if only because she was Giorgio's sister."

"We will save her boss."

"Legs was there with Giorgio's natural father, they've vowed revenge."

"That should put the scare in them and make them fearful."

"But not enough we have to step up our plans and beat them before their reprisal."

"Vengeance is vengeance, boss. Maybe we should let them take each other out?"

"No! I will have my revenge and once more they will know it was me!"

"I'm glad I'm not your enemy."

F rank left and over the next couple of days spread the

gossip in town that Legs and Gambino were gunning for the perpetrator. I watched in glee as or quarry seemed too afraid to leave town they had fearfully looked around for evidence that would lead back to them. I had a letter placed in their letter box at their hotel which said...,

I know you killed the Palmano's. If you want to keep my silence from Legs and not have me allege that you killed the Palmanos, meet me behind the Franklin building Friday at midnight. Bring $50,000. Come alone. If anything should happen to me all my evidence goes to Jack "Legs" Diamond and Paulo Garbino. So, no funny stuff!! I'd sign a friend, but you know I'm not. You'd better pay so I don't stay your enemy.

I had just got back to my room at the boarding house when the landlady told me I had a call answering the phone I heard Frank.

"I've found them, Albert Anselmi, and Joseph Giunta."

"You've found them?"

"Yes, and they're goners by tonight. There holed up in a remote cabin. The isolation of the cabin means that Paul Spano and Detective Alfred Campagna will not find out they Anselmi and Guinta are dead for a few days, not until just before their own fatal blast. "
"When will you be back?"

"Tonight."

"Then tomorrow we set up the flash caps and scare them."

"Whatever you say, boss."

I felt relieved but then guilt crept in. This was real I'd now have blood on my hands but then so did they and they were one step closer to meeting their maker.

Frank went to save Gina, while I watched for Paula Spano, Alfred Campagna and John Scalise, to show up for our meeting from a nearby rooftop. Frank assured me he'd be able to approach Gina, while Scalise was gone and rescue her.

I thought at first the caps set about going off as firecrackers would scare the men; but then I decided it was also necessary to shoot one of them. But which one? I also had to think of where on the body would do the least damage; but sufficiently alarm the men, as I wanted them frightened. Had my family suffered fear? Of course they had and so would they before the final act of blowing them up.

I felt nauseous again for the umpteen dozen time and wondered if I should be so hasty with this plan. Of course I had to do this not only for Giorgio's sake, and my families but for anyone else who could be their target.

I decided on my mark to hit just before they arrived. That bastard, Scalise arrived first and my fingers lingered on the trigger of the Tommy gun as I had in my sights. He looked around cautiously and smugly looking for his new victim who had sent the note. He raised fingers indicating to his men to scour for the note writer.

Damn no Spano, or Campagna, wait a minute there was Spano standing there smirking. I wanted to grind that arrogant Spano's face into the ground. Then I remembered the flash caps. I triggered them with the fuse wire that I now lit. They went off as planned and Spano ran. I shot then rapid fire triggered from the Chicago typewriter spattering bullets everywhere. I aimed hitting his lower leg. Let him suffer I thought.

When they arrived at their car... Boom, no more problem! They'd have just enough time to read my final message of revenge, before their car exploded in their faces. But I still had to get away from the other men and I didn't have much time. I hid the Tommy gun in an airshaft at the top of the building and I ran fast down the fire escape and right full long into Campagna's arms.

"Max Justice? I should have known," Campagna cried.

Dreadful, he knew who I was! Maybe I could bluff my way through this and still sustain my separate identity of Xavier Sword? I'd certainly try.

"Monsieur, let me go you've mistaken me for someone else."

"It appears you're correct I have mistaken you for someone else," Campagna replied.

I breathed a sigh of relief. He believed me. Just then an explosion was heard as my plan went off as planned (minus Campagna of course).

"What have you done?"

"But monsieur you said you were mistaken. I have done nothing but used the fire escape to get way from mon conjoint."

"Your what?"

"My spouse. She yells when I leave to go to the clubs and drink."

"The jig is up Max, or should I say Maxie?" Alfred Campagna announced pulling a gun.

"My name is not Maxie. You're mistaken."

"No, it's Maximilliana Palmano, if I must be precise."

"That's correct and you're about to die you bastard. Just like your colleagues just did," I cried.

By this time I had pulled my gun and had it in his side, but he also had the gun on me. We tussled as he tried to take my gun away and I his rolling on the ground and the guns went off. Blood dripped from a through and through on my side. I glanced at the wound a mere flesh wound.

Campagna bled from his chest yet he still came at me. I crawled to grab the gun he knocked out of my hands, but he grabbed my legs and tried to pull me to him. I kicked back with all my legs force and he let go and I continued to crawl. Just as I reached the gun, I looked back and saw Campagna with his gun in his hands. I heard a bang and closed my eyes waiting for the bullet to hit me.

I felt no bullet pierce me. Why? I opened my eyes to see Paulo Garbino with his gun drawn and Campagna lying dead on the ground, his eyes staring blankly up at the sky.

Paulo Garbino smiled at me and motioned to me to help him move the body. We pulled back the back seat and rolled the body into the trunk of his Desoto, a daunting task with my wound throbbing.

"Get in now, Maxie. Then we can see about your wound."

"It's a scratch."

"Fine, get in Maxie."

I got in the car shaken he knew who I was, but he'd saved me from Campagna. Surely I'd be safe in his car?

The car peeled away from the curb as we drove into the country.

"You know who I am?" I asked as he continued driving.

"You're my daughter-in-law, Maximilliana Palmano."

"But how did you know?"

"I suspected but I knew when Campagna called you by name. My boy did good when he married you, even if you weren't able to save him."

"I thought you didn't care for Giorgio."

"My boy, by Catherine isn't half the man, Giorgio was. I loved his mother, my beloved Sophie, but I foolishly married Catherine in the Catholic Church. Catherine, such a fastidious woman, she still annoys me with her lists and never ending whining. Unfortunately there can be no question of me leaving her, exceptionally after my daughters and son were born.. I loved both my boys, don't get me wrong; but I couldn't take away their legitimacy from his siblings. Giorgio even if he didn't want any part of his father's business, had my heart. Giorgio was a great son and the best part of me, my legacy and those bastards stole that from me, and you," Paulo cried.

Paulo then turned his eyes away to hide tears.

"I loved Giorgio," I told him.

"I know you did and you've been busy getting revenge on his killers."

"How do you know that?"

"My men tell me, that your man Frank and his hatchet men put the drop on Albert Anselmi, and Joseph Giunta this morning. Good work, you aint half bad for a dame. With the G-man Campagna dead in the trunk we've got one less to worry about. But Spano only has a leg wound and Scalise got away."

"Don't worry I have plans for them."

"Do you now?"

"A pipe bomb is on their car and it's set with an alarm clock to go off tonight."

"I planted one in the club where Gina Palmano sings. That's where that bastard Scalise hangs out."

"But what about Gina? Giorgio loved his sister. You can't kill her."

"One of my men will get Gina out in time with a message. Don't you worry."

"So were in this together?" I asked.

"Why not? You've helped dispose of these cretin who whacked my son. We're here time to get the body planted. No careful don't want you leaving any hair behind or any other evidence. We better burn the sucker."

"But won't someone see us?"

"Dearie, this is the middle of nowhere. No one will know that he took the big sleep here then we'll had for a doctor for your scratch before it intensifies."

Two hours later the body still smouldering, we drove back into the city, neither of us wanted to miss our final revenge. Paulo drove me to a building in a broken down part of town and for a moment I thought his words had all been lies, that he planned to kill me too.

"We're here Maxie. A doctor I know has a clinic here."

I breathed a sigh of relief and wandered in behind him. I guessed I did need a couple of stitches as the make shift bandage I'd put on it was saturated with blood and it dripped a bit through my shirt. The waiting room had a lot of people in it some of them coughing and covering their mouths. A few men made me uneasy with their greasy hair and manners. Their hands in their jackets as if ready to reveal a gun at any moment. Then I realized they were just cold. The clinic in a poorer part of town wasn't heated. What kind of person had I become that I could misjudge people so badly.

"Maybe I should have the doctor come to you. Some of these people look really sick."

"Mr. Garbino, how can we help you?" the nurse asked noticing us at the door.

"My friend needs to see the doctor. Is he in?"

"Come with me. I'll put your friend to a room while we fetch him."

I followed the nurse to a room. She demanded I go behind the curtain to put on a gown on my top half. I must have grimaced for she said, "Don't worry we'll keep the secret that you're a woman."

I wondered how she knew, and then realized it was because she was in the medical profession. It wasn't anything insidious but I wanted to get out of here as soon as possible; so I followed her advice and donned the gown.

She left and I waited for the doctor. It seemed a long time before there was a knock on the door and a man walked through. The man came in his hair black and his eyes the colour of coal. His mouth curved into an easy smile and my heart almost stopped. It couldn't be him. I must be bleeding more than I thought to conquer a ghost. He reached out and touched my hand. He was real. I felt faint and before I could say one word I did something I vowed never to do. I passed out.

~0~

My eyes opened a few minutes later to the man examining me with a stethoscope. I looked on him in shock and hope that I truly saw Giorgio in front of me.

"How?" was the only word I got out.

"You're my half-brother Giorgio's widow, Maxie, aren't you?" the man asked, "I'm sorry I scared you, father should have warned you. I'm Doctor Marco Garbino. I know a lot of people thought we looked alike and we are...were close in age."

I still couldn't look at him in the face. If I did I'd start crying he looked too much like my beloved Giorgio. My mind didn't want to separate the two, but I had to ask him the questions that plagued me, "You knew Giorgio?"

"Knew him and loved him like he was my full brother."

"Giorgio never spoke of you."

"Giorgio was afraid to speak of me and get me in trouble with my mother. Mother doesn't know that I kept in touch with him. She wouldn't have liked that. Now I've stitched up your side when you were passed out. Father said you were in some danger from the same men that killed my brother. Are you still?"
"No," I lied.

"You ought to be more careful then, that little one you're expecting might object."

"Did you say expecting? I'm pregnant?"

"It's a guess at his point, but I say you were about two months pregnant. We probably could do some more tests; but I'm a very good doctor and I'm sure."

Amazed, overjoyed and overwhelmed I cried tears of joy and sorrow. All my emotions were pulled to the surface.

"Are you okay?" Marco asked concerned.

"Sorry, I'm happy, but I'm also sad because Giorgio will never meet our child," I explained.

"Neither will you if you don't take care of yourself. I love my father, but I'm under no illusion; he wants revenge for my brother's death. If you're with him danger follows."

"I'm fine, and so is my child. Women have babies and work until the week they give birth all the time."

"But for how long. Do you know why you passed out?

It wasn't just the shock of seeing me. You need to watch your blood pressure and take care of yourself and this child. I suspect you haven't been eating properly. Grief will do that but you have to eat properly and frequently. You must eat at least three times a day, or five small meals so this child will flourish."

"My child will be fine, now that I know I will take good care of him or her," I protested.
"I should tell my father. He'd make you rest."

"Don't you dare! Isn't there some doctor oath that you can't do that?"

"I won't tell him for now, but you have to start taking care of yourself and don't put yourself or this baby in danger. My niece or nephew needs you."

"I'm not in danger."

"Do you think I'm stupid? I heard about a shooting near the Franklin building. That's how you got that bullet wound isn't it?"

"How did you know that?"

"Caught you, didn't I?" Marco exclaimed.

"I have to go now," I said slipping behind the curtain and putting on my shirt and jacket. Then I came back into the main part of the room.

"Not before you get some prenatal vitamins from me. Come and see me at the end of the week. I want to know you're blood pressure is stable."

"Fine."

An explosion noise rocked us off our feet. Marco grabbed me and kept me upright as another rumble came through. The door opened and in walked Gina.

"Marco, sweetheart I thought we were going out for a late dinner," Gina cried then seeing me she said, "Oh, I didn't realize you we're with a patient. I'm Gina Palmano. Wait a minute, don't I know you? You're Max Justice. But I thought you were dead!"

I said nothing and Gina seemed distracted, almost depressed that Marco didn't respond to her immediately and dropped this for a few moments. Gina looked like she wanted to talk to Marco but not in front of me. Just then an explosion rocked us off our feet. Marco grabbed me and kept me upright as another rumble came through.

"Did you hear that weird sound outside and feel the ground shake. Was that an earthquake?" Gina asked.

"Maybe," Marco answered, "Gina, you should have waited outside. I'm with a patient."

"I can see that Marco. But I can keep a secret I know Max," Gina protested, then turning to me she asked, "Tell me Max if you survived is there any chance my brother survived too?"

"I'm sorry Gina, but I only survived because I left earlier then Giorgio and Maxie."

"Sorry, Max. It seems my wife knows who you are," Marco said, then realizing what he admitted he looked scared.

"Marco you just told her, I was your wife. Why?" Gina asked sounding angry.

"Sorry, Gina it slipped out."

"If your dad finds out he'll be furious."

"Maybe it's time we told him; I'm sure he'd be glad to meet his granddaughter," Marco claimed.

What Gina was his wife? That was unexpected and her husband looked like her brother. Yuck! And they had a child? Then he'd have to tell her who I really was. She already guessed I was Max it wouldn't be a stretch to guess that I was her sister-in-law. The gig was up.

"Wife? But your dad called her Gina Palmano."

"You won't tell him will you?"

"We both have our secrets. Don't we Maxie?" Gina stressed to me.

"I won't tell Gina," I answered.

Another loud rumble rocked us, shaking us almost off our feet.

"Did you hear that? It was another boom!" Marco asked. "That sounded close by," Gina cried.

As everyone rushed to the door to look down the street where the sound had come from, Marco looked pointedly at me as if I was behind the explosive noise. I was knocked off my feet and hit my head. I swear as I looked across the room near the door I saw a ghost materialize. As I looked around the room to convince myself I wasn't the only one seeing a shade; I realized all eyes were on the street and the explosion. None of them saw the ghost. It was oddly like time had stilled, as I watched the ghost develop first fuzzy, then a sharper image of a man. It was Halloween today the veils between worlds had opened, for before my eyes Giorgio appeared.

"Maxie..."

"Giorgio?"
I looked around. It was almost like time stood still and no one heard him or saw him but me. I looked back at Giorgio.

"Maxie, you've taken lives. This isn't the life I wanted for you. You can't keep doing this. You must stop."

"I can't. They killed you," I whispered, tears filling my eyes.

"If you keep this up our daughter will die."

"They must pay."

"They will; but not by your hand. Now go. Get away from all of them before it's too late. Trust none of them, except Frank."

"I don't understand. Why can't I trust your sister, brother and father?"

"One or more of them, maybe behind my death. Please Maxie if you ever loved me, flee now. Save yourself and our daughter. Get away now."

Before my eyes his spirit dematerialized and it was like time began again as I heard the conversation continue around me. Surely the bump on my head had made me imagine this... that and my guilt. I didn't see a ghost. Did I?

"Maxie are you okay?" Paulo asked.

"I'm fine."

The club where you sing has blown up, Gina," Marco exclaimed, shaking his head then seeing his father he yelled angrily, "You did this didn't you?"

Paulo looked sheepish.

"You could have killed my wife. How could you?"

"Wife?"

"Gina is my wife; whether you like it or not. We've kept this secret to long."

"You married your brother's half-sister?" Paulo cried, then turning to Gina he admonished, "But how could you? He looks just like your brother. It's sick."

"You better put your old fashion notions aside old man. We have a daughter and if you want to see your granddaughter, you better accept us," Gina declared.

"How old is my granddaughter?"

"Francine is two and before you connect the dots we've been married two and half years."

"But I heard you were with Johnny boy."

"John Scalise, icky, He's promised to help me get a career in Hollywood. I might have strung him along a little; but I couldn't be with him. I love Marco. Marco and I will move to Hollywood in the New Year. John's promised me jobs with his connections."

"That's not what I heard. My man told me you're his dolly."

"Nonsense, I love Marco."

"Quit avoiding the obvious father, you put my wife in danger with your revenge,"
"I didn't put your wife in danger. I made sure Gina had left before the bombs were set off."

"How many innocent people did you whack, old man?"

"None! There were only bodyguards and the men that killed your brother in that club when it blew."

"And you wonder why I didn't tell you were married."

I wondered if I should heed the warning and sneak out while they were arguing. I opened the door and went to go out.

"Where do you think you're going?" Paulo asked grabbing my arm.

"I'm back to my rooms unless you need me more tonight?" I replied hiding the shaking in my boots.

"Yes, I guess it's been a long day. I'll check out the explosion and let you know in the morning unless you'd like to come with me now?" Paulo asked.

"As long as the deed is done," I whispered.

"Where can I find your man Frank?"

"Frank won't be back until tomorrow morning," I lied.

"You room with Sally Andrews's, right?"

"That's right," I admitted but secretly vowed to find other rooms before morning.

"Fine, my man will drive you home and I'll see you tomorrow morning Max."

For a moment outside the clinic, I breathed a sigh of relief that he'd let me go. Then I started thinking his man could drive me anywhere. Luckily for me he dropped me off in front of my rooming house. That's not to say that they went away. They didn't. I noticed three of Paulo Garbino's men watching.

Whose side was he really on? Did he cover up his own actions in killing my husband, or was he really as innocent as he seemed?

I ran up the stairs to my room and noticed the door to my room was ajar. Every noise seemed to amplify, as I heard a slight rustle from someone moving inside. Opening the door with my gun, I used the door to hide behind.

"It's okay Maximilliana it's me."

I couldn't believe my eyes. I had to take his hands in mine, before I believed my Grand-père Bordereau stood before me. I cried as I hugged him; never so glad to see anyone in all my life. My body folded into his like I was a little girl again and he could solve all my problems.

"My darling child. it will be okay."

"But how and is there anyone else who survived?" I asked.

"I wish the others had Maximilliana. It's only by a fluke that I'm not dead."
"A fluke?"

"I hate flying. It's a relatively new thing. It's meant for birds, not people. So when this FBI agent came and said he needed a seat to transport a prisoner I saw it as my chance to take the train to the other plane which would take us to Paris."

"So then what happened?"

"I said my goodbyes and the plane took off blowing up right in front of my eyes in midair. I stood there stunned and devastated; but everyone thought I was dead. I planned to contact you once I got to Stratford, Ontario, Canada, but then I heard you and Giorgio had died and I had to come and see for myself, if it was true. Every contact I had told me it was true, that you and Giorgio had died. I had to see for myself; so I went to your funeral and saw you on the edges skulking. I tried to follow you but I lost you. Then I ran into Frank and he told me you were rooming here."

"Frank told you that?"

"Yes, he's worried about you. Now he doesn't mean to criticize you; but as I said Frank's worried. You've gotten into too tight with Garbino. He doesn't trust him, or any of the others that Garbino knows."

"I don't trust him either. Did you have any idea Gina was married to Doctor Marco Garbino, Paulo's son?"

"Gina's married to him? Ne pas mettre le chat parmi les pigeons. Gina a menti à son frère, j'espère que vous n'avez pas confiance en elle," Grand-père moaned.

"English please, my French is rusty."

"Doesn't that not put the cat amongst the pigeons? Gina lied to her brother; I hope you don't trust her."
"I don't trust anyone accept you and Frank."

"I am glad to hear that. Now I have some bad news. Men watch yours and Frank's rooms. They however didn't see Frank come back and hustle me through Sally's secret doors."

"Sally has a secret entrance? How did Frank know that; if I didn't?"

"Sally and I go way back. In my younger days, I knew Sally We spent hours together."

"But I've never heard you mention Sally," I protested.

"We had a misunderstanding and we spotted seeing one another after five months. Then I met your dear departed grand-mère and the rest was history, until a week ago."

A knock was heard at the door but before I could answer it with y gun drawn in walked Sally Andrews straight into grand-père's arms.

"Did you tell her about the danger were all in Pierre?" asked Sally.

"Danger? All of us? How much does Sally know?"

"Sally knows everything. You see Sally and I were married yesterday," Grand-père admitted.

"Married?"

"Oui, mon cheri. I'm sorry you could not be there."

"Congratulations to both of you," I exclaimed.

They were both older and deserved happiness where they could find it, besides I liked Sally. She had welcomed me when I first come to this city. Her rooms had all been full so yet she found me that first room where they'd bombed my accommodations. She had also warned me about suspicious people around those quarters which had kept me alive.

"I know you had a grand-mère; but I hope that someday you might call me great grandmother Maximilliana."

What could I do? I welcomed her to the family. It was then that Sally explained to me why she'd come to my room. Frank had apprehended some of Garbino's men planting explosives around Sally's rooming house. He'd temporarily disarmed the devices. Now they were set to explode by morning when we'd be gone.

"So we fake our deaths again and we go to Stratford, no?" Grand-père announced.

"But how can we do that again? They'll never be fooled."

"They will. I can find the bodies. I have a friend with a funeral home," Frank said sneaking up on us, "They didn't know our destination; but I suggest we go to the bigger city London and lose ourselves there."

"It's a good plan; but we've only got a few hours and you didn't know about grand-pere and great-grandmother Sally"

"I should I have told you but I want you to see for yourself that your grand-pere was alive. I've already got the bodies on ice boss; an older woman (sorry Sally) and an older man who are about the same size and someone our sizes boss. I knew we'd need to fake our deaths again. Frank stated, "The plan is in play, the bodies are literally on ice in the basement."

Grand-père and my new grand-mère, Sally crept downstairs to the basement to check out the bodies and prepare them for our demise. I had to hurry with my packing and meet them in the basement now as we'd agreed to plant the bodies and leave.

I heard a thundering noise on the stairs, as Gina ran up and into my room carrying a small child which she placed in in her arms. Her face was drawn and huge bruises crisscrossed her cheekbones her eyes were sunken and rimmed with purple, yellow and green. She then slammed my room door shut and bared it with a chair.

"You have to help me Maxie. You have to help me protect Francine from them. Even if you care nothing for me, help me get away and protect Francine, until I do. Please, I'm begging you. Marco and his father want to kill me and take Francine. Marco believes his father lies that I cheated on Marco. For the record I didn't. I loved Marco until today. I never would have believed someone who loved me could do this," she cried.

This was a complication I didn't need but how could I turn my back on Francine or Gina?

"I don't understand you acted like Marco was the love of your life. Did he hurt you?" I asked, knowing full well someone had done this to Gina.

"Hurt me? You can see the bruises. He's so aggressive and threatening I have to get away, but I cannot with Francine. He'll find me easier with Francine. You can take her to safety. I'll meet you anywhere. Please?" Gina pleaded touching her eye and cheekbones.

"You want me to take your daughter to safety? But what about you?"

"I can find my own way without Francine."

"I could help you get away, Gina. You are my sister-in - law."

"No, just take my daughter. I'm going to Toronto. There are some people there who have limited contacts in Hollywood. I'll meet you there in a week at the Arena Gardens in Toronto at nine p.m.," Gina cried placing a bag on the floor and running out as fast she could before I could even blink.

My niece lay sleeping in my arms unaware that her mother had gone. My senses heightened, I waited a couple of minutes then carried her down to the basement.

"Maxie, whose child is that?" asked Grand-père.

I explained and told everyone how Gina needed me to take her to Toronto. We went ahead with our plans and placed the bodies in the rooms setting the charges for an hour from now. We then slipped out the back and to our vehicles. Three hours later, nearing the border to Canada, Frank adjusted the radio and boosted the signal so we could hear the news. Tuning in we heard,

An explosion at a local rooming house has killed four people. In other news the police are looking to question the owner of a black Chevrolet Universal AD. A pedestrian was killed while crossing the street in front of her home. Witnesses say a car seemed to head right for her. Neighbours say the woman was the mother of a small child killed in the rooming house explosion and that she may also have been targeted. Local sources are reporting the woman's name as Gina Gambino, daughter-in-law of rumoured mobster Paulo Gambino.

I couldn't believe it Gina was dead? Could she have faked her death? Of course she could have, we reasoned. We concluded however that we had not been followed and our death seemed believable in the media.

We then rationalized that Stratford, being small, could not contain us safely, people would be quick to gossip about new people in Stratford, so we went on to London.

Frank even confirmed this with his contact at the truck stop. Francine slumbered on not waking, until the car stopped in London. Instead of screaming she kissed me and hugged me calling me Auntie Maxie, only it sounded like Annie May. I wondered how she knew me until Frank told me that Gina had taken the picture Giorgio had of us after 'we had died' and had given it to Francine. She didn't seem to miss her mother. Gina worked so much at the club that was probably the reason why. I only hoped that Francine would continue being so happy. We found a restaurant and ate breakfast like a family. Frank left halfway through to find a place to buy. He came back in a half hour with a deed in hand to a huge mansion in the best part of town.

Settling in, one week later we still went to Toronto to meet Gina in case the rumors of her demise were faked. She never showed. Either she had really died, or something else had prevented her. I never heard from her or Marco again. I heard later that Marco and his father were killed in a drive by shooting two weeks after we left.

Investing our money in different stocks and bonds, (locomotives being a prominent one) we lived comfortably in the mansion. The neighbours all seemed to think, we were the idle rich and we allowed them to think so.

I found my way back to my faith and gave confession to all my crimes asking God's forgiveness. The priest seemed alarmed, but he gave me penitence. He thought I could find redemption. I began to work in the Catholic Church helping those less fortunate have food to eat clothing and shelter while Sally babysat Francine. The priest seemed to worry about how pregnant I appeared; but I insisted on my need to make a difference. Francine soon seemed to completely forget her mother and as I grew closer to my daughter's birth she started calling me Mommy and I didn't discourage her.

Frank had been holding out on me. He had a secret himself. The day before we left the United States he found out he had but a year to live. Frank decided in the time he had left he would find me someone to share my life and look after me because he not only had promised Giorgio to look after me but he too loved me. He introduced me to many men those first six months, but I wasn't interested.

He found a doctor whom he trusted to help me give birth safely and I gave birth to Georgiana. I wished Giorgio could have seen her but Frank did. He struggled with his illness but he managed to wait for the announcement of my daughter. After he greeted my daughter with tears and gifts he went home and that night he passed away.

I wallowed in my grief, even as I rejoiced in Georgie's birth. I'd lost too many people and Frank's death was the last draw for me. The young doctor tried to comfort me. Grand-père and my new grand-mère approved of Doctor John Waverly. The young, handsome and charming doctor wormed his way past my grief and my misgivings and became my second husband. My Grand-père passed away the next year followed by Sally only a year later.

Grief bogged me down again, but Francine and Georgiana drew me out of my doldrums and then John and I added our three boys, Frederick, Colin and Lawrence to fill up my time and life. My life was full and then the war came. I joined the bandage brigade; as weapon making held no sway for me. I begged my husband not to join; but he knew he was needed, and he signed. Frederick followed his father's lead and stole away at thirteen years old to join. I tried to get him back but fate's fickle hand reached out to Fred when the troop boat he travelled on was torpedoed. John was killed on D-day and didn't come home again.

Francine got married at eighteen to Jerrod Travers and had three daughters of her own, Anna, Paulina and Colleen.

Georgiana married Thomas Warden and had three boys Patrick, John and Luke. Colin and his wife Christine had three boys, Hal, David and Derek, Lawrence and his wife Rebecca had three girls, Carina, Elizabeth and Noreen. I now have grandchildren and great grandchildren. My children have become doctors, (Lawrence and Francine) lawyers, (Georgiana) and even librarians of which Colin is one. My grandchildren have found their place on the straight and narrow as well. I have been truly blessed despite my former life of crime.

I told Francine yesterday, my secret, that her mother was my dead sister-in law. She was angry at first as she thought I was her mother. I had also always told her that Giorgio and her aunt had died from influenza. I hope and pray that you, Franny, will forgive me. I did what I did to protect you; but I know now that you deserved to know your roots. To my other children this changes nothing Franny is still your sister, as much as she always was. Embrace her and show her your love through this difficult time for her.

But my time grows to a close, is limited and I must continue my account. I wondered if I should leave this account of my younger years, my crimes, but my family deserves to know. I lived the life of a gangster, with retaliation and revenge. I committed murder and I am ashamed and hope that my maker will forgive me. I hope that you and my dear children and grandchildren can still look at me with love.

Remember that I chose to walk away and give my children the something I never had, stability and no relatives, to lead me into crime. That's not an excuse mind you. I made my choices and I had to live with them. But I gave you all the best lives I could. Please, dear children, don't find the road I once did. That road is filled with nothing but pain, anguish and regrets.

For this is the true story of what occurred all those years ago; for my name is not Anna Waverly, but Maximilliana Waverly, and I was once Max Justice.

~0~

Sucker

Awakening from a drugged sleep I found myself naked, my ankles tied, my hands tied above my head. Groggy, I struggled to untie myself and managed to slip one of my wrists out of its bonds. Slipping the other wrist out, I untied my feet. I heard no breathing and assumed I was alone. The room was dark, but I spotted a thin line of light indicating a door hinge; inching towards the light the walls I felt cold and cement-like the floor smooth and slippery like glass under my feet and hands, and I inched forward.

When I almost reached the spot, light flooded the room as the door opened.

"Going somewhere?" the man laughed, as he blocked the doorway.

"You took the wrong woman," I commented, stalling until I felt better.

"But I thought we had body...er...chemistry," he laughed.

"In your dreams, buddy boy."

"You're all talk, for a naked chick," he stated.

"Am I?" I asked.

He looked puzzled, but then regaining his confidence he said, "You're amusing. This will be fun."

"Yes, it will be," I commented taking a deep breath and transforming.

"What are you?" he screamed horrified.

"You're about to find out."

"But you're big and ugly see-through cloud what can you do to me?" he asked getting his bravado back.

I inched forward swallowing him whole. I then transformed back into a beautiful statuesque brunette. Stepping into the light I found my clothes, leaving no trace of myself behind. Another job well done.

~0~

Trapped in hell

As the police arrived, they found me on the floor, covered in blood. I heard the footstep; the heavy traipses of their regulation shoes; as they came up the wooden stairs and thank god that I wouldn't die.

"There's something you need to know, this one's alive!" the cop declared.

I gave my statement of how my step-father had killed my sister, my brother and my mother and then he stabbed me multiple times; only to have me grab the closest object a pen, to protect myself. The pen nicked an aortic artery and my step-father bled out shortly after.

The inquest was done with, I recovered, but I wondered would I be caught? They deserved to die, I reassured myself! They had all beaten me, degraded and belittled me. I went over every detail of how I had first drugged them all to the gills, (except my step-father) in their evening meal. I had wanted him to feel every minute of the killing for his treatment of me (for which I still bore the scars) but it had backfired on me. The small dose I had given him had meant that he had caught me as I dressed, after exiting his shower to wash off the blood. He had grabbed the knife from me raging and stabbed me, multiple times. I grabbed the pen off his dresser and stabbed him. Then I ran into my room and called police.

The police had believed me. I was safe. I had gotten away with murder, but had I? Haunted at night, I relive it over and over again, trapped in a hell I can never awaken from.

Why am I confessing to you? Because I have a taste for blood now; despite the fact that it haunts me, I hunger to feel that power in my hands again. No, don't run; or do; for it will make it that much more pleasurable. I am at heart a murderess you see, and I belong in Hell; but hey it's lights out time. I'll see you there later.

~0~

Soup' s Up

Stepping onto the restaurant with my killer boots with spiked heels and my favourite jeans, I noticed an empty place. Smiling at my boyfriend and said, "Thanks for emptying the place, but you know he's coming back."

"If Paul comes in here, I'll get him. I have a plan," Derek responded.

"I have a restraining order. I'll slap his ass back in jail," I responded.

"He wasn't in long enough for what he did to you!"

I frowned at him.

"If he lays one finger on you, he's dead meat, Derek raved."

"I can handle him now I have to go to the ladies room," I said.

I'd almost reached the ladies room when a hand reached out and grabbed me. I kicked back as my taekwondo instructor had showed me with my spiked boot and hit the chest of the person. Removing my boot I turned around. Blood poured from the chest wound and I heard the sounds of gurgling and then gasping as Paul took his last breath.

Oh no, I killed him, I bemoaned. But he had accosted me. I didn't mean to kill him. I pulled his body into the ladies room and locked the door. I stood there as a half an hour passed and I heard knocking on the door and Derek's voice.

"Is he dead," asked Derek coming to check on me.

"Yes."

"Good! Henry it's done. She did it herself," he yelled.

Henry the owner came running with a wheelbarrow and then pushed Paul into the kitchen; where he proceeded to use a saw to chop him up. Then he put him in the meat grinder and made sausage out of Paul. Tonight's menu, sausage, kale and lentil soup served to the men's rights group that Paul belonged to. Bon appetit!

~0~

Reprieve

The courtroom hushed as the defendant took the stand.

"Do you sleep better this way, now that your wife is dead," asked the prosecutor.

"Yes, I sleep much better this way," the defendant admitted, "She didn't like me going to bed at eleven. But I didn't kill her."

"I'm finished with this witness," the prosecutor announced.

"Do you have any idea who committed this murder?" asked the opposing council.

"Overruled," the judge said,

The defense lawyer lifted an eyebrow.

"Fine, I'll grant you leeway, but get to the point."

"Poor bugger! Your honor; I have proof that someone else committed this crime."

"Objection. If they had proof it should have been provided before the trial your honor," cried the prosecutor turning a pasty grey color.

"Opposing council approach the bench," the judge commanded and then continuing he said, "Provide the evidence now."

The judge stared reading the evidence provided for a moment and then signaled to the bailiff.

"Arrest the prosecuting attorney now," he demanded.

The courtroom went wild. What kind of evidence could have made them arrest the prosecutor?

The whole story came out a few weeks later. The murdered woman had bullied and beaten her meek and mild husband who had tried to love her. She had then cheated on him with the prosecuting attorney. Blackmailing the prosecutor, and threatening to torpedo his career and end his marriage; she taunted him with all that she knew. The prosecutor killed her and framed the husband. The prosecutor got life, the husband a reprieve; he's happy now with a woman who truly loves him.

~0~

What Cost?

"**W**hat's this?" I asked disgusted.

"It's called a dress, D.R.E.S.S., Virginia," Rea said.

"There was nothing with a zipper?"

"Quit being sarcastic, this is important."

"I know."

The red dress barely covered my breasts and rear. Going to the bar as instructed I sat on the stool waiting for him. Tall, dark haired with flashing blue eyes he was most girl's dream date.

"Can I buy you a drink?" he asked.

His back turned, I slipped the drug in his drink, luring him back to our house. He then passed out in the living room. Rea tied him up with my help and we dragged him to the basement.

"Why am I here?" he asked, when he awoke.

"Remember me?" Rea asked.
"No. should I remember every chick who picks me up?"

"Wrong answer, Drake." Rea said kicking him, "I don't even like guys, but you didn't care."

"You didn't protest and neither did any of the other women I dated. The court didn't convict me."

"No the court didn't, but a bunch of the women you 'dated' are anxious to meet with you again. Come in girls," Rea cried.

I let the twenty women into the room. Drake heard them and blanched, "I'm sorry, I'll never do it again!! I promise!!!"

"You're right, you'll never do it again," Rea responded.

The next day I read in the paper local comedian, Drake Ashburn was found dead in a ditch. Police search for the killer or killers. Anyone with information contact...and I shivered. I had protected my wife, Rea and other women from a monster, but at what cost?

~0~

Money Pit

I sat in my chair at the table just staring furtively,

contemplating slaughter. I hate Brad. I hated everything about him, but especially his constant bitching about what I had to do. I didn't need something else telling me what to do.

"What are you doing?" asked my daughter entering the room.

"I'm thinking of committing murder," I answered frankly.

"Say what? What's got you in such a mood?"

"A lot of things. Could be that it's a Friday the 13th and the moon is in Scorpio a water sign and the new moon leads me to destructive behaviour. After all I may want to get rid of some spiritual and material crap," I quipped.

"Mom, since when have you embraced new age views?"

"Since about two hours ago," I exclaimed tapping my phone, "After all I may want to dig into the deeper mysteries of life and embrace "quality over quantity."

"Did Dad do something to piss in your cornflakes?"

"No!"

"My sister?"

"No, again, I'm just desiring a little better communication with the cosmos," I responded.
"Oh, but, murder... are you sure mom?"

"It shouldn't have to come to this. Like I said I just wanted a little cooperation a little communication, maybe some easy advice...not a contract killing homicide."

"Mom, you're making things harder than they are. As usual!"

"No, I'm not. Nothing is ever so simple as it seems to others."

"But mom, manslaughter? Such a drastic step and so expensive; don't you want to think a little more about this?"

"I'm still debating, or I would have already committed the act," I insisted.

"So you're thinking before you act like you always told me to do. Okay see you later," my daughter said leaving through the backdoor.

"I'll think about it, see you later." I answered, but, really I thought of how much I hated Brad. How much that voice of his grated on my nerves. How I could keep my own notes and information up to date. I'd could communicate face to face I didn't need him doing my talking. I glanced at my phone and in that moment I reached the end of my tether.

"Fade to black, I'm going to put you down," I yelled.

I threw Brad against the wall smashing him to pieces.

Cooling down I realized that the updates for Brad had been that outrageous and now I'd need a new I-phone again. My fifth in the last two years...what would I call this one Money Pit?

~0~

Look-sees

My grandmother raised me, she was tough, but kind. She harped on to me about how young ladies didn't chase after men; they made men think it was all their own idea. She also always had what she called her look sees, remembering all of her prophetic dreams; other times just bits and pieces. The problem with Gran was she manipulate me with her premonitions.

Trouble on the way," she would say and then she became mysterious and she would tell me to stay away from someone. I felt most of her premonitions were a light-year from reality but often I did listen, but only because I cared more about my grandmother than I did the people she warned me about.

The day he arrived, I fell head over heels in love with him. Kale Rannoch, handsome charming, every girl in town wanted to be his girl. Imagine my surprised when he picked me. I didn't share my relationship with my grandmother because I liked keeping it secret and the other reason? I was afraid my grandmother would try to ruin my relationship to keep me with her.

Three months passed and Kale asked me to marry him. He knew I was an old-fashioned girl and he told me he'd wait until marriage to sleep with me. He told me he loved me and I believed him. I was thrilled but now I had to tell grandmother and she wouldn't be happy I'd kept Kale from her. I told her about Kale and showed her pictures on my cell phone.

"Oh, Victoria, when will you pay attention to me? He's the boy I had a dream about. I told you about this a couple of days ago remember?"

"No, I don't remember, grandmother," I answered.

"Victoria, you have to break it with this man before you get hurt," my grandmother began.

"Don't start with your premonitions now. I love him and I'm going to marry him. Who knows in a year or two you could have a great- grandchild."

"Victoria, my dreams have showed he's a bad egg! He's not who he says he is. He's a wolf in sheep's clothing. Do you have any idea what he does for a living?"

I told her I did he was a businessman, and then I stormed out and eloped with Kale. It turns out grandmother was right. Kale wasn't just a businessman. He dealt in drugs and worked for a Mexican drug cartel. His name was Rannoch either, his last name was Caro. We weren't legally married. He was already married to his sweetheart Maria Luisa I quickly found out after the feds arrested him for smuggling and drug trafficking.

I thought grandmother wouldn't forgive me but she was the first one at my door after the cops took Kale away. She's a great grandmother now. I had my daughter last week and named her Moira, after her. I read in the paper that Kale had been murdered in prison. Grandmother just winked and said she talked to an old friend about Kale. As for me I'll always listen to grandmother's look-sees from now on.

~0~

The Mouse Turns

The man had to die he simply had to die. If good people were to survive, I needed to put an end to his onslaught of slings and arrows, his constant mistreatment of his employees. The women he came in contact with and discarded. All condemned him to his fate. I was a quiet sort, seeking the shadows, but even the mouse turns when mistreated. And oh, how he'd mistreated me. It was too much to bear.

He simply had to go. For all concerned he was a monster of epic proportions. Look how he treated the servant girl that tended to him in his bath. She was all of thirteen years old and he had pulled her in his bath. He used her like a plaything, simply there for his use. Then when she turned up pregnant he denied it all. He called that sweet young girl a slut, and had her dismissed, thrown out of the house five months gone.

He treated the cook and the housekeeper like they were his wives. I who to my misfortune to be his wife? He treated me like the scuttle maid. How had I, Harriet Tuttle Pembrooke, been foolish enough to marry such a man? A man who beat me, mistreated me, and took his fill against my will in the marriage bed? Even now I sported a bruise over my eye and purple bruises beneath my dress, and on my chest, my stomach and my thighs. How had I come to this you ask? A rich single heiress, once.

My parents had died and I had been entrusted to an elderly relative who by all accounts just wanted to get rid of me. They sold me to the highest bidder him Lawrence Pembrooke. I had been a mere fourteen years old and knew no man. An innocent child given to a savage man, who took me violently our wedding night and then dismissed me as nonresponsive and too passive.

He took my money and my good nature that night. No longer the happy young woman full of life, I was a shadow, hiding my presence, hoping he wouldn't see me and beat me, hurt me again.

Five long years of being shut in rooms held prisoner unable to leave the home as he used other women he brought to our home. I also was hungry; so hungry. My jailers kept me with little food. Sometimes when they were generous they gave me gruel, most days however I received bread and water. My jailers as I like to call them the cook Mrs. Adelaide Pym and the housekeeper Mrs. Gumm claimed they were widows, but they loved to warm his bed. I didn't even quibble about who shared his bed as long as they both had a chance to. Once they had bragged they had both graced his bed at the same time. I had thought they were welcome too him if he was busy with them perhaps he would forget me. I was wrong. He was insatiable he just took and took, like a greedy pig at the trough. I'd had enough a week ago he had come home in a rage.

With Mrs. Pym's and Mrs. Gumm's help, as they held me in place he had beaten me unconscious. As I took blow, after blow; they smiled in malicious glee. I collapsed finally lying on the bed and passing out. I awoke alone naked and bleeding, as I gave birth to my stillborn daughter that he had thrust from my body. My daughter born beautiful and tiny, her rosebud lips never to breathe air. She was not left in the womb long enough to survive, with me, being only six months gone.

Lawrence had come stumbling back into the room a drunken lout. He stared at her body my Rosalie's body and then had said, "I did you a great favour. Daughters, nothing but trouble and I would have had to drowned or give her away. We need an heir and a spare not a girl. Clean yourself up woman. You are dirty."

He sent the jailers, his co-conspirators in the room to clean me up and they took my Rosalie away. Where I do not know; for I am still jailed in my room, brought out only like a pretty toy for parties. Whether she was buried I know not. I was let out of my room today, only a week later for a party, a party that would take place this evening. As his wife I was nothing, but his chattel no one would help me champion me. If he were to be gone I would have to do it myself in such away no one would suspect me. But how?

Poison, but where would I find poison for a rat. For he was a rat, of epic proportions. He had battened and slimed his way through life, destroying life even his own child but those women were also to blame. The rage in me for Rosalie's demise burnt bright and strong and revenge was the only word on my brain.

The kitchen....I could wear my kid gloves and sneak into the kitchen and find the rat poisoning that Mrs. Pym kept there. If she was blamed no matter she and her cohort, Mrs. Gumm were as evil, as he was. I succeeded in my quest, a small amount of poison now in my gloves waiting for my chance.

I am dressed all in finery hooped skirt lovely green velvet
dress and jewels around my neck, diamonds my mother's
diamonds adorn my neck. I worked as if asleep with no
emotions. I pretended… I smiled like a doll, showing that
all is right with the world. Mrs. Johnson nodded to me. I
nodded back. She's married to his clerk and I must be civil
at all costs. I continued mingling. He is always nearby, ever
watching. I nodded to other women and be oh so polite,
doing the job he expected. I waited until Mrs. Pym brought
in the drinks and bumped the table. I knocked up against the
table unseen and dropped the poison in the biggest cup
waiting there, which Mrs. Pym has placed on the table.

He bades me to him. He goes to the table and I waited
allowing fate to choose his destiny. He picked the biggest
cup, like I knew he would. He drank deeply. I hid a smile.
He continued gorging on food and drink. He has chosen his
fate I've only to wait.

He continued to preen and pimp among the peoples
assembled. Hours pass and I see him holding his stomach
and complaining about gas. He passed the hour's playing
cards and winning from the man assembled; telling me to
go to bed. I am dutiful, am I not the dutiful wife? I do as I
am bid, and a way to bed. I hear the lock click on the
bedroom door. I have my alibi as Mrs. Johnson watched
and noted this misuse.

I sleep and awake to my door being opened by Mrs.

Gumm.

"The policeman wants you," she said showing standing him
behind her.

"Give me a moment to make myself correct," I stated as I
shut the door and dress quickly and demurely in grey
clothes, then came out of the room.

"Mrs. Lawrence Pembrooke? the policeman asked tentatively.

"Yes sir," I replied meekly and demurely looking downward.

"Someone has done in your husband. Have you knowledge of this?" the policeman blurted out.

I paled and appeared to look stressed and frail.

"Have you lost your head Evans? I said I would interview the Mrs," retorted another policeman at the bottom of the stairs angrily.

"So have you been shut in your room Mrs. since last night?" The policeman who was reprimanded asked.

"My husband is dead? Oh no, tell me it is not so," I wailed and then fainted.

As I come out of my pretend faint the policeman helps down the stairs and to a chair.

"So you've been in that room since last night?" asks the lead detective

"Yes sir like a dutiful wife I go to my room and my husband locks me in to protect me," I stated with doe like eyes, and then I cried pretty little tears.

"But who was there to protect him from whatever evil took him away from me last night?"

"It's all right Mrs. We think we have the culprit. Were you aware that your husband had relations with your cook Mrs. Pym and this woman here Mrs. Gumm?" the lead detective enquired.

"I know nothing of that sir. My husband is really dead?

You've made a mistake correct?" I demanded sounding sad, but hopefully that they are wrong.

"I am afraid we haven't Mrs. He's dead." the policeman announced.

"He had relationships with those two the staff has confirmed it. They also say that you had a baby a week ago born dead." the lead detective accused.

"I did indeed my poor daughter was born still and I was very sad," I responded.

"These two kept you locked in that room. They took your baby as well and buried her."

"They only did as my good husband bade. My job as my husband's wife is to keep him happy. Have I failed in that duty?" I asked demurely and with great horror.

"You were put upon you, poor woman," the patrolman cried convinced of my act.

"What were you doing last night?" asked the other man, the lead detective.

"Last night? I was my husband's hostess as we gave a party for his associates in business," I replied truthfully.

"And did you have an occasion to serve your husband drink?" the man enquired.

"I did not serve him he bade me circulate the room and play hostess as he got his own food and drink." I answer "Then her guilt is clear. Mrs. Pym served the drink that poisoned your husband we found the dregs of poison in his cup and you Mrs. Gumm you helped her did you not?" the lead detective addressed the men.

"You say the servants killed my husband? But why?

Why would Mrs. Gumm and Mrs. Pym do such a thing?" I asked with tears in my eyes.

"Mistress they wanted the master. I saw them fawning on him as they locked you in your bedroom. When they summoned me and bade me get drink two nights ago they were naked in his bed," my husband's manservant said to me.

I feigned shock and disgust and hide the anger I feel for them killing my Rosalie. The lead detective seemed convinced and took Mrs. Pym and Mrs. Gumm to Newgate prison.

The trial takes place a month ago many of the other servants testify of their long term relationship with my husband. Testimony has been given of an argument that took place outside his bedroom two nights before the murder. Their fate was sealed with their lies, they will swing by the rope until they are dead.

For a moment I feel guilt and then I realize they met their just reward for killing my Rosalie. Two months have passed since the trial and yesterday the hanging took place. I moved away to the countryside to live quietly. No man shall possess me or dominate me ever again I have my money and my freedom. And my tormentors and Rosalie killers have met their just fate. I live my life; no guilt shall engulf me. I am free, happy at last.

~0~

April Showers, Bring May Flowers

"And how are we today April?" asked the voice.

I'd learned to dread.

I answered "Fine," because I thought if I didn't bad things would happen. I still puzzle why I am here in this sterile white walled place... but never aloud, the one time I did the repercussions were not something I wanted to repeat. Somehow a padded room and a jacket were not at all comfortable. I realized the man had been droning on and I had not heard one word.

"April why are you here?" the voice in the white coat asked almost sighing

"I wanted a vacation spot?" I spouted my heart beating fast

"April, we talked about this. You use humour as a defense mechanism but we need to talk about what happened the night of May tenth."

"Nothing happened," I answered quickly, I would never tell anyone what happened that night, not ever. I bit my lips as if to keep them from speaking.

"I know you are scared but you need to talk about that night to get better. Trust me April am your doctor and I need to know what happened to you in order to help you."

"I don't want to talk about this," I persisted frightened if I talked about this it made it real. Reality was not a place I cared to live.

"April, I'm sorry but you make it difficult for both of us. We have to get to the bottom of this in order to resolve your difficulties," He persisted injecting something into my arm.

I felt myself floating way from him deeper inside my own body. From far off I hear a voice say, "Why do you persist in this doc? April is an innocent she wasn't there that night. I was."

I was puzzled someone else was there the night Jerald died? The only thing I remembered from that night was the blood that clung to my shirt and somehow got on my hands. I also remembered the rough treatment from the police before I passed out and found myself here in a padded room dressed in a strait jacket. Was this the person who killed Jerald? I wanted to see them but this deep sleep the doctor had put me in kept me trapped only able to listen… and so I did some more.

"What is your name?" the doctor asked sounding surprised.

"May," the voice answered.

"And what is your purpose May?" asked the doctor.

"To bring flowers," laughed May.

"I don't understand," commented the doctor.

"I was the observer," May answered.

"Was? Never mind, let's move on to the same question I asked April."

"What's up doc?"

"What happened on the night of May 10th?" asked the doctor.

"Happened? Why Jerrald, the rat died!" replied the voice.

Jerrald was a rat? What did this voice go on about? They obviously didn't know Jerrald well. He had his faults; and yes he was a little too sharp at times. Perhaps a little too easy with his temper but he loved me. I know he did and I loved him. Jerrald had loved me despite the fact that I was a mouse and liked to hide in corners in social situations.

"Jerald like the attention he got with April on his arm. He liked that she appeared shy and retreating, so other men would escape her notice. She eluded sweetness. She appeared as trusting and loveable as he saw her, but he slowly eroded her confidence making her a mouse, hiding in corners lest she offend him," May said angrily

"And what did you do about this?" the doctor asked.

"I? What could I do? I stayed silent until I was needed," May answered

"But you didn't stay silent did you, and that made matters worse for April. Didn't it?"

"I couldn't stay silent. He harmed her," May answered.

"How did he harm April?" the doctor persisted.

"She cried."

"She cried? When and why did April cry?"

"So many times she cried. When he would go out at night and come home smelling of other women. She cried," May responded.

"So he cheated on her. Did that make you angry?"

"I was angrier when he hit her gave her black eye and broke her arm. She cried then, too," May answered and I heard anger in her voice.

How had she known of Jerald's cheatings and his beatings of me? How could she have known? I told no one. She spoke of a broken arm. I had no broken arm and I didn't remember a broken arm. Yet my arm did ache in the cold and damp. This was curious.

"Does April know about you?"

"April know of me? Not likely is it. How could I protect her if she knew?"

"You protect her then? You don't allow bad things to happen to her?"

"Didn't I just say that?" asked May.

"Did you protect April the night Jerrald died?" asked the doctor.

"I did, Jerrald tried to kill her. He wasn't going to stop that night."

"Tell me what happened," begged the doctor.

"April was excited. He had promised her a night out. She bought a new dress and had her hair done," May began

How did she know all this? I wondered trapped in my slumber.

"She thought she would finally get a marriage proposal," she continued, "Frankly, I was dismayed. I thought she should leave him not marry him. He however had other plans," May answered.

How did she know this? Did I know this May? I didn't remember meeting any May. And what was this about Jerald? He had been going to propose to me I know he was.

"Jerald had found another woman he could manipulate better. He decided to kill April."

Why did she lie about this. Jerrald would never hurt me, I thought. Then I thought back to all the times he had hit me and given me a black eye. He had hurt me. Could she be telling the truth? No, Jerald wouldn't kill me. He didn't have another woman.

"Jerald began by placing the plastic on the floor. I saw him. She was to step on the floor and then he would shoot her but I removed the bullets."

"You knew and just removed the bullets?" the doctor asked

"Oh no, not at first. I suspected he planned something when he put the plastic down, but only when I saw the bullets being placed in the gun did I know. I took them out, but even that didn't help."

"Why didn't that help?" the doctor asked curiously.

"He had a back-up plan. He had the knife he planned to chop her up into little pieces with it," May explained.

"So what happened?" asked the doctor.

I couldn't believe what this woman said about him. I wanted to leave this fog I was in and shout she lied. Jerrald wouldn't try to kill me. Why did she spin such elaborate tales?

"What happened? I observed him. He raised the blade to strike her and I fought back. I grabbed the knife and when we were fighting it went in him. I think it struck his heart. Appropriate don't you think he eroded her heart and I eroded his."

She had killed him. She claimed to save me; but I didn't remember seeing her. That night was a blank. Could she be telling the truth?

"And you left her to face the police?" the doctor asked.

"I couldn't stay. I stepped out my job was to observe, not kill. I couldn't handle it. I called the police and left," May answered.

"Do you think April knows?" asked the doctor.

"She does now. April's been listening as we speak. Tell her I'm sorry, I had to protect her."

She knows I'm listening? How does she know that? I wondered.

"April I did all to protect you. We are important, worthwhile, and loveable. Don't let Jerrald's behaviour destroy you," May stated suddenly talking directly to me.

I began crying inside. I didn't understand what had happened, but it made me sad.

"Why do you cry, May?" asked the doctor.

"I'm not crying April is."

"April cries? Does she understand what happened that night?" asked the doctor.

"I told she listens. You are listening aren't you April? She is crying again .I must take charge and protect her," May announced.

I understand now May is in charge, because I let her be. I couldn't handle life, so she helped me. This conversation happened months ago and still I hide in darkness, May needs to be in charge and she's living my life. The doctor keeps trying to intricate us, but I am reluctant. I enjoy hiding in the shadows, letting May fix things. May is stronger and wiser than I. She won't let anyone harm us. She keeps my tears away because April showers bring May flowers.

~0~

Judgement

It was an act of mercy. I had rescued others, including my Angel, by snatching him to the flames of judgment.

He tormented my Angel. He cheated on her. He believed he could do whatever he wanted with no consequences.

My Angel had cried as he beat her; cried as he tried to turn her child against her. If only I had been there to save her in those ten years he spent with her. I spent those years trapped in a world of his making, trapped in his shadow.

I scurried from post to post, always in the dark. My Angel had been brave, but she became a shadow of herself. She too trembled, in the thunder of anything that moved. She looked at even me with fear.

I condemned him to a fiery hell and yet he still tried to escape. Didn't he know I would do anything to stop him, even kill him? He protested, oh how he protested.

Excusing himself with tales of childhood trauma. Didn't we all bare the pain and trauma of childhood? Why did he think that excused his behaviour? He used his fists on those lesser than he Did he think I would excuse that behaviour?

I looked through the glass at him. He seemed harmless but I knew better. I would keep him in the flames of judgement he wouldn't escape. I was his judge and jury.

I heard them but I ignored them only hearing their voices as they talked softly. I needed to keep my wits to keep him prisoner.

"The patient seemed agitated today, should we up his dosage of Thorazine?"

"Yes, another episode like yesterday would be most unfortunate."

"What is his story anyway?"

"His neighbours complained to the police about an obnoxious smell from his apartment. The police responded to find him holding a decomposed body of his wife. When they investigated they found a small child dead in another room, food piled up beside the bed. The weird thing they had been dead for ten years. They judged him and sentenced him to a mental facility for life."

"How did he explain his crimes?"

"He screamed and cried that it wasn't him. He claimed his twin brother had committed the crime."

"Does he have a twin brother?"

"He did once, but he killed him about the same time as his wife. They found his body in a closet."

Nonsense these people were mistaken I wasn't dead. I existed within him, keeping him in the flames of judgement; and he would never escape my judgement.

~0~

The Kids Are All Right

Mary watched as George made the kids lunches.

Didn't he trust her to make them anymore? He just seemed to go through life in a fog anymore ignoring her.

"George, let me make them please. You made a mess of that sandwich. Frannie doesn't like it when you make the jam squeeze out the side, and peanut butter? Really, George? You know the school has banned peanuts because of student allergies. I can do it with ease if you'd let me."

"Daddy, we can't eat that. Peanuts are banned. Sheryl has a peanut allergy. Just me taking that to school could kill her." Dara complained loudly, "Frannie can't take that either. Gee Dad, you make sandwiches all backward."

"I did try Dara. I'll try to remember that omission next time." George promised

Gee, he wouldn't even look at me when I complained; but he jumps when Dara complains. It was like they didn't have a relationship anymore. The only thing that seemed to be keeping them together was the kids. He didn't even yell like he usually did how odd.

"Go tell your sister we leave in five minutes for school," George demanded angrily, "I can't be late for work again. I'll lose my job."

"If you'd let me drive them like I used to you wouldn't be late," Mary sniped.

George just stared into space and ignored her after Dara left. He then proceeded to ignore her some more.

"George listen to me! I have to go to work soon. I could drive the kids you don't have to worry about being late."

George doesn't answer and Mary gets annoyed.

"Gee, George, I make one small mistake and you won't talk to me?"

"Dara we'll be late." George shouted. His hand reached out to hit Dara but then he pulled it back.

"Fine then I'll quit the job. I know you want me to be home for the children."

George just seemed to nod at his head, while not looking up from the newspaper he read. George then proceeded to the front door to get his shoes ignoring Mary.

"I know I was wrong to do that George. I'm never going to do that again. Why won't you forgive me?" Mary demanded.

"Damn you Mary! Why did you make me do this?"

George asked

"What did you do, George?" Mary wondered aloud.

Just then there was a knock at the door. George opened to a police officer. Two uniformed police officers came in along with a woman dressed casually.
"George Barnes?"

George just nodded. One policeman then took out his cuffs and put George in handcuffs behind his back.

"What's going on? Why do you arrest me? I have two kids upstairs you know," George complained.

"George Barnes. you are under arrested you for the murder of your wife Mary Barnes, on May second of this year. You have the right to remain silent and refuse to answer questions. Do you understand? Anything you do say may be used against you in a court of law. You have the right to consult an attorney before speaking to the police and to have an attorney present during questioning now or in the future. If you cannot afford an attorney, one will be appointed for you before any questioning if you wish. Do you understand? If you decide to answer questions now without an attorney present you will still have the right to stop answering at any time until you talk to an attorney. Knowing and understanding your rights as I have explained them to you, do you wish to answer my questions without an attorney present?"

"I didn't kill my wife and what about my children?" George asked again.

"Mr. Barnes we are aware of your children. Ms. Albert from social services will take custody of them."

The policeman then took George away.

Mary at first wanted to deny it. She wasn't dead but when they started reading George his rights, she remembered. She remembered the beating she took from George. Thank goodness the kids hadn't been home but at her mother's. George had yelled at her for forgetting to make the reservation. She had made one but they had lost it.

Would he listen? No it was like every other time she should have walked away. He hit her first blackening her eye. Then he knocked out two teeth as he broke her jaw.

He just seemed to never lose his rage that night, no matter how many times she begged and pleaded he just kept hitting. She remembered becoming unconscious then waking up barely to him chopping her bodies into pieces then fading away.

"The kids... would her kids be okay? They must never be with George," Mary thought.

While Mary had been thinking time had passed and she found herself in a courtroom a jurist stood up.

"In the murder of Mary Barnes, we find the defendant George Barnes guilty in the first degree," said the Jurist.

"George Barnes you have been found guilty by a jury of your peers. I sentence you to twenty five years in prison," the judge stated.

"Twenty five years, my life was only worth twenty five of his?" Mary asked disgusted to none in particular.

Mary then found herself floating in time and space to her parent's home.

"Paul, I just got the call. The grandchildren will remain with us not George's parents. We've won," she heard her mother say excitedly.

Mary smiled the children would be safe with her parents.

She turned and saw and outstretched hand in a luminous light. In her head she heard, "Come Mary, it's time you rested and got well."

Mary wanted to go the light was so bright but she didn't want to leave her children. Then she looked and saw Gabby and Dara sitting beside her mother smiling and happy. She knew then she could say goodbye. The kids were all right.

~0~

Spectator

Ilook around me shaken had I really survived a fall from a building so high up? I look around and spot a crowd.

Where are the news crews? I'll see them soon, after all I have survived a fall from twenty storeys and when I look at myself not a scratch is present. No broken bones at all.

I feel euphoric. I was on track for promotion and with the right lawyer I could make him pay. After all, the company stood responsible for my suffering too. They would pay for what I lived through.

Then I look around the crowd gets bigger and they stare at the ground, not me where I stand. What's wrong with them? Did someone else get pushed from that ledge?

Had I grasped the man who pushed me hand too tightly and pulled him with me? Now that would be justice, he tried to kill me after all.

The day had started out so well a new job, a promotion. I thought that Billy would leave his wife for me. He said he said something to tell me to meet him on the roof after work. I like the fool I am, I had done just that.

When I reached the roof Billy told me that it was over.

That I would never marry him. He wanted me to leave the firm; in fact the promotion I had gotten this morning had been rescinded. Tomorrow I would be let go all because he wanted it.

I threatened him with the employment standards board and he laughed at me. I told him I would sue him for wrongful termination and sexual harassment. He laughed again and then he grew angry. I ranted that I would also make everything clear to both the partners and his wife.

Next thing I knew he shook me and threw me from the roof. But I had had the last laugh I survived. Alive I make him pay, just maybe he was the one dead on the pavement that they all stared at.

I inched towards the crowd pushing my way through. I stare down and see something that can't be. I have no job no hope no salvation. It's truly over. There is no hustle no bustle. No track to get back on. No lover to leave his wife. I had my time in the sun the corporate world at my feet. The hurt that I felt at his cruelty was a memory, time had passed and left me behind while I stood there staring.

The light beckons its hand outstretched to me and I realize I am a spectre no more of this world. I lie dead on the pavement. I stared intently as I recognized my battered self. Come, says the voice in the light beckoning once more. I looked back once more at what was my life and then I stepped into my new reality in the light and am known no more.

~0~

Mirror, Mirror on the Wall

He stared in horror at the body. What had happened?

He remembered going to bed taking an Ambien and waking up to blood on his hands. Now there was a dead body next to him. He jumped out of the bed and stood beside the body. What if he had been responsible for this? He noted they were dressed in nice silk pajamas like his. No they were his. So he must know this person. He starred long and hard at the face. He knew that face but who was it? He gasped ran to a mirror. Looking back at himself he cried. Why?

~0~

Phoenix

She stumbled away from the fiery wreckage broken and bruised but not burnt. How was that possible? Elaine didn't know, but then she didn't understand a lot of things about today.

Some men had kidnapped Elaine off the street near her college. She didn't even know them. Who were they and what did they want from her? They kept asking her questions about where Elaine was born and who were her parents? She had been a foundling; she didn't know how to answer their questions. They continued driving Elaine away further away from her home into the desert.

She begged them to tell her where they were taking her but was met with only silence. The PlastiCuffs the men used on her chaffed her wrists and ankles. They didn't cover her eyes; so it was obvious to her from the moment they snatched her that they wouldn't ever her go. One drove the van and the other two yelled all the questions.

Elaine pleaded telling them she would forget all about all of this, if they'd just let her go but the questions and the slaps across her face, began again.

"Do you suffer from blackouts? Lapsed time? Do things move around you without the use of arms? Do you have any unusual unexplained abilities? Elaine had no idea of how to answer. These were the strangest questions she'd ever heard. She wasn't a super human. She was just a normal eighteen year old woman, going to college and working at a coffee shop to pay the bills. If she had super abilities she wouldn't have to work so hard.

One of the three men started hitting her harder. She could feel her cheeks bruising and her eye swelling. The strangest thing happened, she felt like her tissue repaired itself, like it had never been injured in the first place.

She grew frightened and then very angry. Before she even knew what happened the cuffs melted from her arms and legs. Fire shot out from her fingertips. Fire from her fingertips... no one could do that and yet she had done just that. No one could heal that fast either.

Who were her parents?

The fire continued growing in size and the van blew up throwing her free. She was alive and she had not a scratch on her. She had done the impossible that is why these men wanted her, but who were they? The government? Were any of them alive? No matter what they had done to her she could leave them to die. Elaine stumbled over to the wreckage. With great remorse, she realized all but one of them had perished dead. Elaine advanced on the third one carefully, than realized he too lay dying.

"What did you want with me?" Elaine asked him "You were genetically engineered by government scientists to be the perfect super soldier. You have abilities that normal humans don't. We were hired to retrieve you now that you're an adult and your power is about to erupt." The man answered.

She left him to die shortly after that. Elaine walked to the next town caught a bus to the nearest big city. She then went to the nearest drugstore, where she bought hair dye to change the colour of her hair to flame red. Elaine took a driver's test in the name of a dead child and then got a passport and flying to Alaska to hide. There she lives a quiet life in the wilderness. She has neighbours who she might say "Hello" to but she remains a solitary figure.

A short time ago a government official found her and tried to approach her. Elaine warned him off with deadly accurate fireballs that fell at his feet. Neighbours say she is happy; but the government watches her still. I know because I am the van driver that survived and she is my job. At least that is what she was supposed to be. My boss thinks I live in town and keep watch over Elaine but I live at Elaine's. Soon I'll have to quit and reveal that we will be married and they will send someone else.

But they better realize Elaine and I will do anything to protect her. And when I say anything that is what I mean. So, if you are the agent sent to watch us watch your back and don't make any sudden moves on Elaine, or me, or you will be toast.

~0~

He Had It Coming

Tears streamed down her face as the gun clattered on the ground. "I just wanted to know who I was."

"Tell me the whole story." demanded the detective.

"I was found a year ago with no memory of who I was. Beaten and in a coma for some months I lingered in twilight. Then he came. Every day he came. He seemed so nice he was an orderly and he would come and visit me. He read to me and at first it didn't register .Nothing registered except the noise of the machine breathing for me and the endless sleep. Then slowly I awoke to hear his soft voice reading .You wouldn't know what that's like to be reborn that way... to see the world like a newborn babe."

"This isn't telling me why you shot him." the detective protested.

"I'm letting you know what happened," she objected "Fine then continue."

"I came alive. I looked forward to him coming every day even though I couldn't speak not then..."

"What happened then?"

"I fell in love with the man who told me the stories. He told me such glorious stories of love and happily afters."

"I still do not understanding the reason why you shot him. You just said you loved him."

"Oh I loved him but I hated him."

"I don't understand make me understand."

"He seemed so charming, so incredibly sweet he cared for me or so I thought."

"But you moved in with him when you left the hospital."

"I know I did but that was before I knew the real him."

"You talk so cryptically. Are you sure you don't need a head doctor lady to put your head on straight?"

"My head is as clear as it can be now."

"Tell me the reason then why did you shoot him?"

"He changed once I moved in, He was angry at the slightest things. I thought it was my fault so I tried to be nicer but he grew angrier. Then he would buy me flowers and say how sorry he was to yell at me. I still didn't remember the past but he said that didn't matter. I just wanted to remember my name. The hospital called me Jane; but I knew that wasn't my name."

"So why did you shoot him?

"He hit me and blackened my eye and that's when I recalled him doing this before. He was the reason I couldn't remember. I asked him why and he said I made him. I shook my head no but he insisted that it was my fault. I asked him what was my name?"

"He laughed and said, "Your name is mine to know and I shall keep it and you.""

"I said I would leave and begged him again, threatening him with the gun. It went off and as he lay dying he said..., "I'm sorry Melanie.""

"So you can see it wasn't my fault, I just wanted to know who I was." I tell them as they placed the hood on my head. Now I feel the drugs course through my veins and I declare, "He had it coming!""

~0~

Gossamer Threads

I awoke from the dream, again the sixth night in a row.

The woman stood by my bed, night after night, blood dripping down her arm, pooling at her feet. Skin, gaped at the neck of the woman and blood oozed from the wound like a geyser. Each night only gurgles emitted from her lips, not words. I reached out feeling tendrils that held her to the earth.

Fear gripped me, my heart beating fast, as I shook myself awake. I picked up the phone and called my psychiatrist. An hour later stretched out on his sofa. I watched as a nurse came in and then I explained it all yet again and he asked, "What did these tendrils feel like?"

"They feel like velvet, or silk gossamer threads," I answered.

We talked for a little longer or rather he spoke nattering on and he sent me home again.

She came again that night her eyes looking downcast and sad. I reached out for her and my hands went through her. Then I noticed for the first time how much she looked like me.

Her mouth opened and I heard what she said for the first time, "I'm sorry, I couldn't save us."

I looked down at my body and realized what I had not grasped from the first. This was my spirit. It had split in two from me since the night we were murdered. The half of my spirit that stayed wandered still mistaken believing we were alive. I felt the pull as we became one.

"Come," she said and we walked into the light.

~0~

Stronger than a Serpent's Tooth

I never imagined he would be the greatest threat to mankind and my undoing...

But I must begin at the beginning, before you can understand why I did it. Maybe it was the foster homes and the lack of love I encountered as a child, but I had wanted all my life to be a mother. Other girls dreamed of fabulous careers. I dreamed of being a stay at home mother, with a house full of children to nurture and shower with love. I would raise my child with praise and encouragement, not punishment. My child would achieve great success and be a source of proud for me.

The reality however was quite different I reached the age of thirty single and childless. A career as an executive assistant, I was happy in my chosen field, but still I longed for a child. I decided to select a mate to give me a child. He didn't have to know. The man would be a one night stand. I fulfilled my objective and Henry was born nine months later.

In the beginning, Henry stood as a great source of joy for me and then sorrow; for as he grew older, he was given to periods of anger. He would lash out and I would scold but he was never really punished, I couldn't hurt that child, the way I had been hurt. He was brilliant and had head for the sciences. It started with a chemistry kit I gave him when he was only seven, and went on from there, winning science award, after science award.

Henry was awarded a full ride to college, because of his brilliance at sixteen. At nineteen, he graduated with two degrees. He then was recruited by the government. I was overjoyed; my son was successful brilliant and now had a career with the government.

Henry was supposed to keep his career and discoveries secret but he could never keep his triumphs from me.

Henry showed me it all his plans, which he had not revealed to the government yet...a bomb worse than the H-Bomb that could destroy most of the world with a push of a button from your living room. I pleaded and begged Henry not to create this monstrosity; but he said it would be his ticket to a page in history. I tried again, but he wouldn't listen to me, only visions of glory in his head. I never imagined he would be the greatest threat to mankind and my undoing, but there it was before me. I waited until he went to sleep and then I smothered him humanely in his sleep. It will do you no good to keep demanding the plans, I destroyed them too.

You don't believe me? Check for yourself his computer information was erased, and then I destroyed the computer. I'm tired now and dying. You didn't know? I took some pills before you picked me up. Henry and I will be together again, reunited in our death.

Goodbye, cruel world you're safe again.

~0~

Death By Misadventure

"Let me get this straight, you and your friend chased a leprechaun and tripped down the embankment. Fell into the culvert, face first, and your friend drowned in the shallow water," I told my partner.

"You're joking. You can't believe that?" Brennan retorted.

"Oh, I believe that one drank too much of that green beer, and then he and his foolish friends all thought they chased a leprechaun." I answered.

"So explain this to me," Brennan demanded.

"I scrambled down the embankment to get a better look going into the long dark tunnel. A few seconds later I came out and saw a leprechaun," the man we were interviewing explained, "I wish I'd been drinking some green beer because here's the leprechaun."

Sure enough there was the green sprite himself. Brennan looked like he was going to have an apocalyptic fit.

The leprechaun came out grumpy and sullen saying, "You disturb me rest again? All I wanted was some Guinness to wet me whistle but I forgot the craiceáilte people come out their shells on St. Patrick's Day. Is it me fault da crazy Sassenach followed me back to me abode? He kept asking for me gold. I suppose you'll want the same, coppers?"

"No, just an explanation about his death," I demanded.

"Now you look like a reasonable sort. I'll call you Sean."

"The man called you by your name," Brennan commented.

"Let the man answer Brennan," I silenced him.

"That there man and his friend chased me down the embankment, fell into da water, afore I could pull him out he was gone. I said me prayers and summoned the likes of ye."

"But he said that he summoned us," Brennan commented.

"He lied!" I answered.

"So how will we write this up?" asked Brennan.

"Death by misadventure, just another St. Patrick's Day for the record. No mention of the wee folk we wouldn't be wanting them to think we were drinking the green beer," I told my partner.

I then wrote the same in my casebook.

"Thank ye kindly youngsters. Come in me shanty, for some Guinness," the leprechaun offered.

In we went. After all who turns down Guinness on St. Patty's day?

~0~

Money Rules, Partner' s Drool

"No doubt about it's a murder," Brennan said starring at the scene.

He seemed too curious by half. It would behoove him to listen to his police partner; before someone silenced his curiosity. I surveyed the scene. Ever since we'd seen the leprechaun he'd been pain. Too curious for his own good.

"All I see is a woman, who had some kind of seizure, fell down the stairs, right on a groundhog; then wander in, then she collapsed and died," I surmised.

"Someone was out to get the woman not the groundhog. They pushed this woman; she hit her head as she fell on the groundhog, Sean," Brennan persisted.

"You make it sound so farfetched," I responded, "It's a simple accident."

"Hardly! The twist is I've traced it back to magic," Brennan persevered.

"To bad, I've liked you as a partner. But the truth is money rules and partners drool," I said raising my hand.

My partner seized and died. A wave of my wand and I had two dead groundhogs. I'd collect my money for killing two groundhogs now.

~0~

.

The Child on the Milk Carton

He had it coming. If you knew him, you would know, he had it coming. He had always been my stern autocratic, dictatorial father. Demanding and perfectionist, he disciplined me when I didn't live up to his standards. I had always had a nagging feeling about him like he really didn't want me but kept me only for my mother's sake. He was physically and mentally abusive, and hard to live with. When I asked my mother how she had met him and came to have me all she would do is mumble. I decided as soon as I could I would get away from him and take her with me but how could I when she seemed so afraid of him.

When I tried to penetrate the layers of deceit, I discovered the truth. I wasn't my mother's biological daughter, or his either. I was a child on a milk carton.

But I'm getting ahead of myself.

I asked her about my birth and she changed the subject. I enquired about my baby pictures and was told they were mysteriously destroyed in a fire. She didn't know my first word, or when I first walked. Things were not adding up and it wasn't like I could ask him. But I put this out of my head until I had to go get my driver's licence. I had demanded my birth certificate for the umpteenth dozen time and had been told they'd have to apply for a new one since mine was lost in you guessed it… the fire. Weeks went by and still no birth certificate. I finally got the nerve to ask him for it.

He yelled, he blustered on about my disrespect of my mother and him and sent me to my room. The next day he woke me up at six a.m. and produced a birth certificate. I took that to get my beginners driver licence and the clerk at the licence place said to me, "I'll give you a break kid. I can't believe you thought this would succeed. Using fake id to garner a government document is fool-hearted. I should call the cops. But you look like a nice kid, so I'm not going to."

"I don't understand," I protested.

"Give it up kid. The gig is up, unless you want me to change my mind and drag you to the cops?" she persisted.

I left then. I was afraid she would call the cops. I tried to understand why my birth certificate had been forged. I then started thinking about all the times I'd asked questions and got vague answers. I'd look at my blue eyed blonde parents and wondered how they could have produced a brown-eyed blonde. How could I have been so foolish? We'd taken this in Biology. Two blue eyed people couldn't produce a brown eyed daughter. Either I was adopted or… I had been stolen.

I went home and began searched forums and missing children's faces on the internet. Sure I wouldn't find anything I continued looking. After all mom wouldn't have stolen me and father didn't care enough to have taken me. Mom wouldn't have stolen me and Father didn't care enough to have taken me. Two hours later there in front of me was the proof a picture that looked like me. It had been on milk cartons across the country. I read the few details on the internet could this really be me? I examined the picture from every angle. I recognized my eyes and the tilt of my head and even then my crooked smile. There could be no doubt... it was me at two years old. I was shocked no wonder my pictures had begun at two years old.

I read the details...

Missing Cecilia Everett
Parents Louisa and Carl Everett 91cm tall weight 13kg
Last Seen in Arva, Ontario on July 12, 1995~At Roundtree Park

I continued reading if you have seen this child call 1-800...and some other numbers that blurred before my eyes.

Where was this Arva? These people were my parents? I had been stolen? There had to be some other explanation. I decided to demand answers from my so called father. I printed off a copy of the missing child flyer on my printer and placed it in my purse.

In a few minutes I arrived at his office building. I swept past the guard at the desk and went straight to the elevator pushing the twenty-fifth floor. Once there I went to the desk where his office his secretary ushered me into his office.

"What's up Lorie?" he questioned, "Why are you here?"

"Is it true? Did you take me?"

"What do accuse me of this Lorie? I have sacrificed for you slaving away at my office year after year and you come to me with these suppositions? You're mine," he declared.

"Read this!" I cried, throwing the flyer on his desk and watching him closely

He unwound the sheet of a paper and I watched as he turned pale and then he burnt it in front of me with a lighter he pulled from his desk drawer.

"Yes, this child looks a little like you Lorie. But don't be ridiculous, it's not you. You are our natural child. Haven't we given you everything you've ever wanted or needed? Put this foolishness aside," he commanded.

"Why did you take me?" I persisted.

"I've had enough of this. Stop this foolishness now. I need to get back to work," he commanded again.

I picked up his desk phone.

"Who are you calling?"

"I will settle this once and for all," I insisted, dialling nine-one-one.

"No, you are not," he cried, grabbing my arm then continued pleading, "Think of your mother. She doesn't know. She thinks we adopted you. She would suffer. Do you want to reward her with jail time? "

I have to admit I was torn for a moment I loved the woman who thought she was my mother. I hesitated and he grabbed once again for my phone. We struggled and moved closer to the window. He grabbed at me again. I fought him and we went sailing through the window falling to the ground below.

As I said he had it coming. I however did not. He had taken me from my family, so he deserved his death. No, I didn't die, but I was in a coma for three long months and hadn't been able to tell anyone my discovery. Then to add insult to injury my ability to speak was impaired when I awoke.

Weeks of intensive therapy and I began to make myself understood. Now I was sure I could tell them what happened. I was worried about my Mother though. She had stayed by my side through of this, her love shining over me, always encouraging me to get better. Torn, I considered letting sleeping dogs lie but I needed to know who I was and where I came from. As I struggled to say the words, in my great stress nothing but a mumble came out. I looked up in surprise as my mother motioned for a couple to come in my room. The woman stood my height and had blonde hair and brown eyes; the man was tall over six feet and had brown hair with brown eyes.

"Lorie, I know what your father did now. I didn't know then. He told me we adopted you. I would never have taken you from your parents."

I took her hand in mine and patted it showing her that I understood and still loved her.

I'm sorry he hurt you. Lorie, I didn't know at all. I really didn't you have to believe me. Oh, I'm not explaining this well. I know you found what he did. Cheryl, your father's secretary finally told me what really happened. She's confessed to the police too. She took you that day on your father's orders, "she paused here, dabbing her eyes appealing to me, "I couldn't have taken someone's child. I thought you were my adopted daughter and you always will but this couple are your real parents. Robert took you from them. This is your real Mother and Father, Louisa and Carl Everett. They have kindly said I could remain in your life and they wouldn't prosecute me for your fath...er...my husband's doings."

"Cecilia my baby," the woman said reaching for me crying no longer able to contain her emotions.

"Mother?" I managed to croak out and am enveloped in her arms and his.

It feels odd and they pull back sensing my feelings. The woman pulls out a photo album of my baby pictures and tells me how she prayed each day to see me again. She reaches out to my mother and tells her they don't blame her. I am happy but still feel a little aloof from this woman. Maybe somehow I can find a way to love the man and the woman who are my real parents.

Weeks later I've recovered I can now walk and talk. I live with my parents and learn more about them each and every day as well how to love them. My mother has moved to Arva to be close to me in fact she bought a house next door. I thought they be angry at this after all she had me all these years, but they are special people who love me enough to share me. I've grown to love them both. They tell me that they love me and they will always love their Cecilia Lorie Everett. They never stopped loving me. Life is good; I am no longer the child on the milk carton.

~0~

A Thief in the Night

I awoke with a start as its dark shadow hovered directly above me. It came like a thief in the night as its tendrils; long bony fingers grasped my neck and tried to choke off my air. I gasped, sputtering as its grip grew tighter. I tried to fight back but lay frozen on the bed. As my eyes opened and took in the sight I saw her. She was a hideous old hag; her wild red blood shot eyes starred at me intently as her long gray hair dangled down over my bed. As her mouth opened, in one smooth movement she sucked and seized the breath that was mine. She propelled herself ungainly, face first into me. As my body absorbed her, I screamed, I shouted -- to no avail.

She found her place in me and she planned on staying. She managed to change my appearance to hers. I scream and arms pin me down tying me to my bed.

"The mirror isn't supposed to be there. It's the Alzheimer's. In her mind she's only twenty-five," said the woman to other woman dressed in the odd polyester pant suit.

"Should we alert the doctor?" asks the other woman.

"No, she'll soon go back to thinking she's twenty-five years old again and be happy," the other woman answered.

I tune them out for I am at peace, she's left my body. I'm young again.

~0~

The Road Not Taken

I don't know how I got in this situation. Such indecision on how I got here. I guess it was fate. Well I guess that's a lie, this morning started out so simply just like every other morning on my honeymoon. That's correct honeymoon number one. I had two. But I'm getting ahead of myself here. A newlywed, fifty-two years old and I was sure I'd found my soul mate. So two days ago we were married.

My husband Brad said he had a surprise for me. He'd made plans for our honeymoon. I was so pleased. I thought I would have to pay for the honeymoon, since I was the one with all the money. Brad told me he had a surprise and wouldn't even say where we he'd take me until we got her to Kaiten's Bluff. It's a remote area way up north. I was surprised all right. I hate the great outdoors and would have liked the option to not partake in them. However when I thought about I was sure Brad had decided to visit the great outdoors, so the press couldn't follow our every move. That's what happens when you are a wealthy socialite; they follow you around looking for the money shot.

Brad tenderly made love to me not once, but three times this morning and then stated that after breakfast he'd like to explore the area. I dithered and complained I didn't have any hiking clothes or boots and Brad gave me another surprise. You guessed it hiking attire. Marriage makes you consider things you've never tried before so I consented. After all hiking couldn't be as bad as I thought I had the right clothes now after all.

After a big breakfast served at our lovely bed and breakfast
we started the hike. There were trees everywhere and I
asked Brad if he was sure he could find his way back. He
then told me to watch as he marked the trees with a
florescent marker. Finally after an hour's trike we reached
Kaiten's bluff. It was glorious there although I didn't want
to get close to the edge with my fear of heights. Brad took
me in his arms. He tried to coax me to the edge.

"You're missing the best part. Look at that blue sky and
those bluffs and if you look way down you can see the
stream. See." he concluded turning my head so I had to
look down

As I looked down I had to admit it was a lovely sight just as
I felt Brad's arms pull back and push me over the edge of
the bluff. I grab out trying to save myself and manage to
grab Brad's leg. We both go tumbling over the edge. I lose
my grip on Brad and he falls to the stream one hundred feet
below. I however manage to grab alone tree that jutted out
of the cliff and with strength I didn't know I possessed I
pull myself up almost to the top to a ledge there.

So here I sit waiting to be rescued two days later. Did Brad
try to kill me? If he was then he's did a good job. Without
telling anyone where we were going, no one would find me.
I'm a sitting duck here waiting for starvation, or thirst to
kill me. I hear a noise a rumble of rocks above as they
petered down on my head.

"Mary-Ann Potter? Are you there? I heard.

I shouted back, "Here, Here."

I am rescued as the person pulls me up with his rope to safety. I look over and can't believe my eyes. It's someone I haven't seen in thirty four years. My high school boyfriend.

"Why George Andrews, I haven't seen you since high school. What brought you here?"

"At the moment rescuing you," George laughed, "I'm sorry Mary but we found your husband, Brad dead, yesterday. He must have fallen off trying to help you."

"He tried to kill me," I told George bluntly.

"You married Potter's son. I thought Potter was rich and left it all to him when he died last year."

"Henry Potter had some money, but Brad squandered it all. Brad claimed his father was in debt at his death risky ventures. Somehow now, I don't believe that," I replied annoyed.

"That's why we broke up high school; I never wanted you to believe I only wanted you for your money." George stated, "I always thought we were soul mates, but you married Brad Potter, a few days ago obviously you weren't pining for me."

"You moved away and life goes on even after nearly thirty four years," I rebuked.

"Has it really been thirty years?"

"You never could count. Did you really expect me to wait forever for you?"

"I guess I did," George admitted.

"George Andrews admit it you were a fool. I married Brad because he was young and he reminded me of you, but obviously that was only skin deep."

"You did?"

"I did. Oh, George, you foolish man, you threw away thirty four years we could have been together," I scolded.

"I'm not waiting any longer," George cried taking me in his arms, hugging and kissing me tight.

"Mary Hatch, I love you," George replied, "You are my moon and stars."

"George lassos the moon," I conceded as his kiss then deepened muffling my speech.

All this happened two days ago. I should have taken this road, years ago. Here I am a newlywed again; married to my soul mate. George Andrews. What a great situation to be in.

~0~

Specimen

He could hear them breathing in the dark room,

sudden sounds of people moving ever so slightly, hit his senses.

When he had awakened a few minutes ago, he had been surprised to find himself here. He could shout but he didn't want to ruin the surprise. He loved surprises did they know that? Darkness lifted with the sounds of something being ripped away above his face. Realization came to him that he had been lying prone. He felt them unwrap him from his bindings.

"An splendid specimen, perfectly preserved," the man cried ignoring him.

"What dynasty do you think he was from?" the other man asked.

"Perhaps the third or 4th dynasty of the old Kingdom?" answered the man.

Zanakht felt searing agony as his chest ripped open and ruptured with a knife, the man held. Then more throbbing nerve ending torture as his ribs pulled back. It was then that Zanakht realized someone had sabotaged his eternal life. He had been a jackass to trust Hapy with his eternal life. They had not removed his heart and organs, only his vocal cords and his ability to move. His heart still beat in his chest, but not for long. Pain blistered into his brain and he begged for release from the soldering anguish that had overtaken his body.

"That's odd. I thought the heart was beating," the man claimed.

Zanakht's sight narrowed even more to a pin of light and he smiled. No pain, no sorrow, just joy. He'd found his eternal life. He'd beaten his enemy, Anubis had saved him.

"A great specimen for the museum." the last thing his body heard.

~0~

Genie in a Bottle

Walking along the beach I saw a bottle glinting in the sun. Part of the bottle appeared cloudy, so in picking it up, I rubbed it on my shirt. A man came out of it in a cloud of smoke. I was excited this could be my big break "So you're a genie? You don't look like one," I exclaimed.

"You don't look like a writer, but you are one aren't you?" the genie responded amused.

"I write under a pseudonym."

"Is that really the story you wish for yourself? No glory, just a name no one knows?" the genie asked "I need to change my cover, to make more sales and promote myself a little more."

"What if I could give you admiration, millions of book sales and immortality?" the genie offered sounding sincere.

"What would that take?"

"I owe you three wishes it would take all of them," the genie explained.

"Okay, then that's what I want," I replied.

"Then say it."
"I want admiration, phenomenal book sales and immortality."

The genie granted my wishes. I should have thought about what I asked for. I got the admiration and book sales. The immortality wasn't quite what I thought it would be; leaving the beach I was run over by a bus and I died. My book sales soared after my death and my book was republished in my name. I became a best-selling author of a children's classic, so I got my immortality. The lesson here is never trust a genie. If you ever find a bottle on the beach throw it back in.

~0~

Forever

She had kept her promise she was back. Olivia put her key in the lock and turned it entering the house quickly. She looked around all was quiet in the house. Olivia was glad to be home but tired from the long drive. She swept up the stairs and went to bed.

"Livie you're here. You're finally here. You've been away so long I missed you," Olivia heard waking from a sound sleep.

"Mere?" she asked.

"Yes, silly. Who else would it be! I'm so glad you're home. Will you play dolls with me and games and...," Meredith rattled on.

"Later. There is lots of time," Olivia answered.

"Please, Livie," begged Mere.

"Okay then one game of hearts, after my shower. I still have to go into town and get some things."

"But you're coming back, right Livie?" Mere pleaded.

"Yes, Mere."

Olivia passed the next hour with Meredith playing hearts with her sister and even giving in and playing Barbie's.

"I have to go honey, but I'll be back," Olivia promised.

"Don't leave Livie. I'll be good, please don't leave me again," implored Mere.

"I'll be back, I have this dependence on food you see. So I must go buy some," Olivia joked.

"You're funny Olivia."

Olivia went out through the kitchen door, but her parents sitting at the kitchen table never even looked up. Arriving at the grocery store, Olivia went up and down the aisles picking up cereal, bread, cold cuts and fruit.

"Olivia Hunsuckle. Well as I live and breathe, how nice to see you again."

"Hello, Mrs. Franks."

"You've been gone a long time. I'm so sorry, for what happened to you," Mrs. Franks stated, looking like she searched for something in Olivia's face, she couldn't quite see.

"Yes I have been gone awhile," Olivia replied, not committing herself. Olivia really wanted to get away from Mrs. Franks, as she was a known gossip.

"Would you like to borrow my iron? Your skirt rumpled from all that travelling you've done. Now, where was it, you said you stayed?" Mrs. Franks continued probing.

"I didn't say where I was staying, but thank you Mrs. Franks, I'll be fine. I don't need to borrow your iron. There's one at the house. I have to go now." Olivia replied politely.

Olivia then went to the check-out paid for her groceries and got into her little red Hyundai. She stared at the old church in the square as she passed it. So many memories there of her and her family, going to Sunday services there. She passed the public school she attended and glanced over quickly at it. She remembered playing on the school ground with her friends and skipping during recess. As she rounded the bend near her house, a truck came at her and she had to jam on the breaks and swerve to avoid it hitting her.

"Whoa, close call." she thought, as she continued driving arriving home a few minutes later.

Entering the house she went to the kitchen hoping to get a glimpse of her parents once again.

"Mom ? Dad?' she called

"Olivia?" her mother asked sounding surprised.

"Olivia?" her father enquired.

"Daddy? Mommy? Oh I'm so glad to see you." Olivia uttered.
"Oh, Olivia." Her father stated sadly.

"We're glad to see you too honey but we didn't think we'd see you so soon." her mother replied.

"Why? I visited this morning."

"Did you tell her yet?" Meredith asked excitedly.

"Tell me what, Mere?" questioned Olivia.

"Hush, Meredith. Let your sister adjust to this," the mother bade.

"Adjust to what seeing you as ghosts? I saw Meredith this morning, when I woke up and then I saw both you and Dad in the kitchen, this morning," Olivia explained.

"You have to tell her Laura," Olivia's father exclaimed.

"No," Laura, Olivia's mother argued whispering loudly.

"Just tell me and get it over with," Olivia demanded.

"How much worse could it be, then you all being murdered, when I was at summer camp?"

"This is worse." Olivia's father claimed.

"Daddy, it should make her happy .She'll never ever have to go away again and she can stay with us forever." Meredith pronounced.

"I don't understand you, Meredith!"

"I'm sorry Olivia the truck hit your car," began Laura.

"No, it didn't. I avoided it."

"That was two days ago Olivia. You've been dead two days," Her father answered.

"I'm not dead. You are all dead, don't confuse the issue."

"I thought you'd be happy, now you never have to go away Livie. You can stay with us forever," Meredith cried happily.

Olivia didn't want to believe them, but as she thought about what they had said, she found herself reliving the accident. Her little red car went around the bend and the truck came straight at her. She jammed on the brakes and the car swerved, but the truck kept coming. She felt the bending metal protruding into her body and heard the grinding sounds, the shattering of glass, as her head hit the windshield. The next thing she knew, she stood outside looking in at the crumpled car. She peered in and saw a body lying there bloodied and battered. They had told the truth she realized as she floated back to the house.

"Oh good, you're back let's play Barbie's," Meredith replied, taking her sister's hand. "Now we can all be together forever."

"Yes, Mere! Forever," Olivia agreed, climbing the stairs to Meredith's room and smiling.

~0~

Forgiveness

Damien the playboy liked his life. He loved playing
the field and sleeping with any woman he chose to.
His twin brother Aaron however was a man of a different
kettle. Aaron sat at home night after night wishing he could
meet the one. Damien loved his brother and wanted to see
him happy so he devised a plan to trick Aaron into meeting
him at a bar after work. Aaron wandered into the bar and
knew at once what Damien was up to and said he was
staying for one drink then leaving.

"Come on Aaron you'll never meet her if you don't get out
of the rut you're in," Damien declared.

"Fine, I'll stay for an hour then I'm out of here," Aaron
declared.

"Wow, look at that chick in the devilish red dress."

"She's pretty, but the devil never created that," Aaron
answered.

"Are we talking about that same woman?"

"The blonde in the blue dress?" asked Aaron.

"No, the angel in disguise with the red hair and the red
dress cut to strategically to show off her best assets, that
rear and those boobs. I like to rub myself all over that."

"You're a pig Damien," Aaron exclaimed.

"And you've been out of action too long," Damien declared.

"I'm not like you Damien. I want a home and family."

"I might want that someday, if the right girl comes along. Be right back got hit the head."

Damien then left. Aaron stared around the room nursing his beer maybe Damien was correct, he needed to start dating at least. It was then he spotted her again the woman with red hair only she'd changed her dress to blue and it was more demure. He walked over to her table.

Aaron was smitten as the woman spoke to him in a Marilyn like voice. Damien too was smitten as it turned out the woman in the red dress was her twin sister Melody. Soon they spent all their time with the women instead of each other.

Aaron grew cold to his brother because Marilyn said he chose Melody or him and he saw less and less of his brother. Damien believed that Aaron had chosen Marilyn over him as that's what Melody told him. The twin men grew more and more distant from one another.

Marilyn's siren song kept Aaron captive he craved her touch as her fingertips and her sexual prowess made him feel invincible and the only man that could please her.

Melody also sent out a siren song that kept Damien in her web. Melody was better he felt than any other woman he had bedded he believed. She was the only one who could please him.

The two men became estranged from each other as it turned out the twin women hated each other. Their father had died from cancer but both women believed if the other twin had only attended the father he would have lived. In fact they had been arguing only a few minutes before and they had decided to never speak to one another again.

Aaron married Marilyn and Damien married Melody. The two men were miserable except when they were in bed with their wives. They missed one another but didn't dare speak to each other lest their wives withhold sex. The feud continued to the men's dying day.

As the two went to the heavenly gates Saint Peter met them asked "Why do you not speak to each other?"

"Because Marilyn's not speaking to Melody and he abandoned me," answered Aaron.

Damien answered, "Because my wife doesn't want me to and he abandoned me."

"Do you not have your own will? Do you condone hate especially hate between family that God himself has picked to be together?"

The two men felt ashamed and admitted so to Saint Peter.

"Don't tell me tell each other," he said.

The two men hugged one another asking each other for forgiveness. Saint Peter then opened the gates to heaven. Melody and Marilyn died soon after and they too came to the gate. Saint Peter asked them the same question. Melody insisted it was all Marilyn's fault. A boy had smiled at Marilyn and not Melody. Marilyn insisted it was Melody's hate. The hate had burnt a hole in both their hearts severing their relationship forever more. Neither would forgive. Saint Peter refused them admittance and they took the elevator down wishing that they had forgiven the transgression that started it all.

~0~

Freedom can be fleeting

It began as the love affair to end all love affairs. At least at my part it did. I loved him with the bloom of first love, not seeing through the weeds to the flowers. I was eighteen, but emotionally I was fifteen, still with hopes and dreams of happy ever afters as I moved in with him.

I had expectations that were never met. He rarely brought me flowers or spoke flowery words. He didn't introduce me to his friends or relatives. He claimed he had none. He took me to dingy cheap places, when he took me out at all. He preferred that I didn't leave the house, lest some other man smile at me. Despite the fact that I rarely saw anyone and would never flirt, or care about anyone else, he accused of cheating. He made my life miserable, but I took the blame. I told myself it was my fault I shouldn't have smiled at the grocery clerk. I should have had the dinner ready when he came in the door. I should have made myself more presentable and not have worn the sweater he disliked; I told myself as he beat me so bad I ended up in the hospital. And yet I still protected him not telling them who had done this to me. I told the police officer who asked that I was mugged. I don't think they believed me, but they let it drop.

Pregnant and overjoyed, deciding to tell him in the evening; I opened my mouth to do so, but he demanded silence that evening. The next morning I ventured out to my doctor's appointment, and I saw him with her. She was blonde and buxomly. He kissed her openly on the street and she returned it wrapping her leg around him. It was indecent and yet a part of me knew this wasn't new. I had been a fool of epic proportions. I must have yelled in surprise for he came charging at me and yanked my arm dragging me home tell me how I embarrassed him!

At the house he demanded to know why I was out of the house. Did I meet a man? I was so obviously cheating on him he went on. I protested and told him I went to the doctor's office. He ordered me to tell him why. I told him about the baby expecting him to be overjoyed, instead he became outraged. He kicked me and beat me and I felt the life in me die, as I began bleeding.

Battered, bruised, and broken, I waited for him to fall asleep. I crawled across the floor from where he had left me.

Grabbing his shotgun from the closet, I loaded it quietly waiting for any sound. I took it into the bedroom and shot him in the head. I was free. That is when you came in response to the neighbour's complaint. I'm ready to go now officer.

~0~

Hell hath no fury

The water dripped a steady rainfall that sent streams of water in rivets across the shallow grave. As I stood over the burial place I said a prayer; but the umbrella I held was useless to prevent the deluge that coated me and drenched me to the bone. I shivered as the wind raised and howled a mournful sound. Henry had it coming. His life had been a well calculated series of incidences where he harmed others to gain his wealth...not one kindness could be displayed in his defense.

As a boy he tortured other children his age robbing of their toys to see them cry. Graduating from that to steal lunch money and then as an eleven year old dealing drugs. Soon a kingpin, attending college and dealing, meeting the right sort of contacts and starting another business calling itself a bank (no more than loan sharking) creating where ever he dealt and yet still accumulated wealth.

Possessive and cruel he acted like he owned his wife, Mara and son, Henry junior, as he told them how to dress act and behave and kept a mistress They tried to escape his grasp, but were brought back by his henchman and then severely beaten for their so-called transgressions. They lived in misery, self-doubt and were but shadow people under his watchful eye.

Henry expected the boy, his only child to follow in his footsteps and often accused Mara of adultery saying the boy Henry junior could not be his. Henry had given them both an extra beating last week for this as he drank his scotch and counted his ill gotten money. That day Mara achieved the courage to leave Henry and take her boy now twelve years old from his evil grasp. Mara waited until Henry passed out raided the safe and took the cash there and a pistol she placed in her purse. Mara now had thousands of dollars as she left with little Henry.

Henry caught up with them first he kicked Mara then blow after blow fell shattering her cheekbones her jawbones her arms her legs; shattering sounds crunching and deafening with their intensity. Henry begging pleading his father to stop to no avail; he only received some backhand blows himself to his eye socket. Henry Junior reached into his mother's purse and handed the gun to her to end to Henry's tyranny. They hastily buried him where he stood. Too bad Henry never learned hell has no fury like a woman.

So here I stood granting the ingrate's last wish to see his burial place and as the rain pelted down I saw a coyote digging at the shallow grave and tear what was left of his body to shred and ingest it. The horror on Henry's face was a boon to me; at last he had met his fate. I, the Archangel Michael could escort him to his hereafter where he could suffer the torments of Hell that he'd made everyone else suffer his entire life. Sometimes days my job made me feel like I served justice and this was that day.

~0~

The Secret of My Success

Dear children, as we are gathered for what is my hundredth birthday, I'm going to tell you a story... the story of the journey of my youth, my children. It all began when I was brought before courts at the Old Bailey in eighteen hundred and sixty two. There people from my youth testified against me. These people who never really knew me, who only knew my father, condemned me in front of the courts. They told of my incorrigibleness. What did that word mean anyway? They said that I was naughty and would never change. Didn't they understand that people change as they got older? Hadn't they? Yet there I sat, locked away with the dregs of society simply because they'd misjudged me.

Oh, my lawyer had tried all kinds of tactics but in the end those people who testified against me were on the zenith of their lives .Who wouldn't trust them over the son of a career criminal? The judge had condemned me and had said I must not commit other crimes, or I would end up like Dr Edward William Pritchard. (He had murdered young women and they had taken and examined his skull after death.)

Had I committed such a crime? *No, I did not!!*

I committed the crime of hunger. I was ten years old and my father had abandoned me to my own devices. I slept on roof tops. I tried to get work; but no one would hire me. I was too tall for chimney work and too skinny for other work. Hungry and without food for a week, I took a piece of bread from the baker. Then sentenced quickly I found myself bound in the bowels of a ship, bound for Botany Bay. I was an indentured servant sentenced to work for some person for seven years. I'd heard at that time that some prisoners were never set free and I was afraid that I should not survive even this. I also heard wild stories that some prisoners got their own land and become free of the shackles of their poverty. Rats filled the bowels of the ship, food and water was scarce. People died around me and were thrown overboard. Yet my life was precious to me and I struggled to obtain what I could and live.

I was taken to work at a station in the outback. I worked hard and the mistress of the station grew to know me. She mothered me and taught me how to read and write. She taught me manners and decorum. Her husband took me into his office and taught me bookkeeping and station management. My sentence was up, but I did not leave, they seemed like family to me. When my mistress' husband, died I was a young lad of seventeen. The mistress had no children. She made me manager of the station. We became an extremely profitable station and my mistress grew wealthy. My mistress lay on her death bed and I grew fearful. I feel like that young boy again. Her lawyer bade me come to her bedside.

"George, my dear boy. You have been a son to me," my mistress said, her words thready as she gasps for breath.

"Mistress conserve your strength," I begged.

"George heed me. You have been a son to me. My end draws near."

"Mistress, no," I begged afraid of losing her and my position.

"George, listen to the lawyer and know I loved you like a mother." my mistress said and then she died.

"Your mistress thought well of you George Smith. She said you were a fine man. Prove her correct make her proud. She has made you the new owner of this station," her lawyer explained to me.

I was stunned. But I did do my mistress proud. I became the most profitable station manager ever.

Now I am an old man my grandchildren, and great grandchildren around me. Once I was a poor slum boy; but I achieved what few can and now at the zenith at my life I can tell you the true secret of my success. Children the true secret of success is hard work and kindness. Not only your own, but what others give you. Be kind and share your good fortune. If you have been blessed give back tenfold. That is my advice for you at all. So, go eat my birthday cake, and remember the roots from where you came as you make a success of your life. I love you all.

THE END

~0~

Thank you for reading this story. If you have enjoyed these stories, please think about leaving me a few words of review at your favourite retailer. Please read on for a sample of my murder mystery A Penny Saved A Murder Earned on the next page.

Sincerely S. G. Lee

Synopsis of Book Excerpts

on the next few pages

A Penny Saved A Murder Earned:

The Kelly's (Lily, Rose (Lily's daughter), Great Grandma Katha and Amelia (Lily's cousin) all feel like they are under a curse; but it appears it's the work of a serial killer that people around them having been falling like dominos. Now as someone is killed at Amelia's store and others known to them perish, Lily and Amelia become under suspicion by the investigating officer Emmett Rogers. They must fight the impulse to blame the curse and get to the bottom of who caused all their woes, before the killer targets them.

A Diller A Dollar A Really Dead Scholar

Lily Kelly, her adopted daughter Rose Brooksfield, her Great-Grandma Katha, and Amelia try to get over their trauma at the hands of a serial killer. Rose tries to overcome the whispers and innuendoes at school by joining in on school events such as basketball and choir. Rose and her friend Carol arrive early to school to participate in choir only to find the choir teacher; Mr. Scholar has been brutally murdered. Rose collapses and is brought to hospital and Lily learns more than she wants to know about Alexander Scholar as she's drawn into the investigation. Now Lily must help Emmett, and his new partner Kendall Owens, find the killer before he or she, threatens the Kelly clan yet again.

If you like to read more of this book or one of the others in the Kelly Murder Mysteries series they are available in paperback or kindle at Amazon.

Dreams Can Kill

Disoriented, memory loss, anger, pain, and fear; some of the emotions amnesiac Sharron feels after a six month coma caused by a head wound from a bullet. Her doctor seems to know her, she has friends, that claim to know her; but who can she trust when everyone around her seems suspicious? To save her future and retrieve her memories Sharron fights to recall through her dreams lest she learns Dreams Can Kill.

Please read an excerpt from *A Penny Saved A Murder Earned, A Diller A Dollar A Really Dead Scholar, Dreams Can Kill* on the next page.

~0~

Excerpt from A Penny Saved A Murder Earned-Chapter 1- Bloody Shoes

"A penny saved is a penny earned" ~ Benjamin Franklin

The blood streaked across the floor, but he had carefully sidestepped it. Stupid bitch! She got what she deserved. How dare she defile his Angel's property? He hadn't left a trace...had he? No, he was too clever by half.

A voice he didn't recognize interrupted his thoughts, "I didn't spot you entering. Working late, dear? Of course, I forgot; you have an early opening tomorrow."

The man strode closer to the killer and the body lying on the floor, "Wait a minute, you aren't the lady. Who are you? You shouldn't be here," the man continued clearly alarmed.

"You shouldn't be here either," the murderer insisted.

"You, you killed Megan. I'm telling."

"Really? You know this was something you shouldn't be allowed to see."

"I'm leaving. I didn't notice anything," the man lied, witnessing the blood.

"I'm sorry pal. Wrong place, wrong time!" the killer answered.

The homeless man ran dodging racks, finally deciding to hide behind some shelving. The killer ran after him, puzzled for a moment because he could see no trace of the homeless person. The murderer then laughed, as he realized how foolish the vagrant was being, his stench gave him away. He subdued the man with a Taser gun. Waiting seconds he then pulled the man from his hiding place. Taking ties from within his pocket; he fastened the man's arms and feet. Satisfied that the homeless person was now trussed up like a turkey, he smiled.

"P...P....P...Please! I don't want to die!" the man cried, visibly sweating and starting to shake.

The man tried to kick out his legs and arms but failed.

"You've heard about fate? Well sorry but this is your fate, buddy!" the murderer explained.

"P...P...P...Please, I'm begging you! Couldn't you let me go? I won't tell! I'll move to another city. Besides who would listen to a homeless man?"

"Someone would. My Angel would."

The homeless man then smiled as if to gain trust from this killer, "You won't hurt the lady who owns the store, will you?" he asked.

"I would never harm my Angel. How dare you?" the killer responded outraged.

"S...S...S...Sorry! I didn't mean to insult you! Please just let me go. I'm harmless ask anyone...."
"What is your name?"
"Why do you need my name?" He asked looking puzzled then reconsidering he answered, "My name is Al."

The killer put his gloves back on and smoothed them and then turned his back on his victim.

"You're going to kill me now. Aren't you? Just don't harm the sweet lady who owns this store. Will it hurt?" the man asked resigned.
"I would never hurt my Angel. She is sweet isn't she? Unfortunately that also makes unscrupulous people take advantage of her."
"I promise I would never take advantage of her kindness. I wouldn't!!! She's the best part of my day and this city, Happy Valley, Ontario. She picked me up from the gutter and helped me."
"I know you wouldn't and it hurts me to do this. Tell you what though, I'll make your death painless because I like you, Al," the killer offered, feeling suddenly sorry for the man.

Then he checked himself. Living on the streets was hell; maybe he was doing the guy a favour? Yes, of course he was. Taking a pill bottle out of his pocket and opening the dispenser, he placed some in a coffee cup he took from the sideboard. He filled the cup with the tepid coffee from the coffee pot, stirring the pills in rapidly.

"C...c...c...couldn't you let me go? I won't tell and I'll watch over her when you're not here."

"Sorry, times up, Al. Here now, drink this coffee," the assassin commanded placing the mug at Al's lips.

Al tried not to drink and spit some of the coffee out, but the assassin plugged his nose and the cup was soon empty.

"Admit it Al, you had a crappy life. Just give in and go to the light. I hear good things wait there for people like you," the killer stated.

Al tried to fight some more, but he soon found it was losing battle. Al's breathing slowed as he slipped into a deep sleep and stopped breathing altogether. His age and living on the streets made the pills work fast.

Now what to do with the body? The killer thought. His Angel must not find this man's remains here, bad enough he left Megan's body here for his Angel to find. He couldn't hide Megan though she needed to be found. Every needed to know she suffered for her crime. Maybe even his Angel would see Megan's evil and protect herself from people like that. This man, Al however knew his Angel and she cared about him. It was so like her to look after the homeless. He could let her cry over Al. Where could he put the man so he wouldn't be found?

The dumpster of course...the perfect place for Al! The day after tomorrow was garbage day. Covered in garbage no one would find Al.

~0~

The next day
Lily

Ominous clouds replaced the morning's sunlight turning the skies to shades of deep purple and navy blue, streaked with gray. Lily Kelly stared at the sky for moment, and then departed the courthouse doors in Happy Valley, Ontario, Canada, skipping down the steps. The city looked its age of over a hundred as the buildings downtown looked old and decrepit. If only the town could find some money to fix downtown Lily thought.

Then her mind turned to Amelia, her cousin and best friend. Amelia needed Lily to support her in her grief. Lily had a fight with her husband Horace again this morning about how much time he was spending at the office and how much time she spent supporting Amelia. Lily was always working, and so was Horace, so how much time was Rose their fourteen year old daughter really getting?

Lily had won in court, but all she could think about was her family. Everyone needed her and she felt like she was being pulled in three different directions. Something had to give and it looked like it was her job. She would have to cut back on some of her work. Her family had to come first.

Lily stumbled some more over the steps only stopping from hurrying across the courtyard to her office, when her heel broke on her shoe. Today was supposed to be about her victory after her win in court; but it appeared with her expensive shoe's heel breaking, she was mistaken. They ought to get the ruts in the paving stones fixed; that was her reflection as she cursed her bad break. What did they say about omens? Maybe she should have taken a hint from the heavens' darkening? She noted as her bad luck had seemed to get worse with the arrival of some reporters.

"Ms. Kelly, give us a statement about the Rockwood case?" yelled one reporter.

"Ms. Kelly, how does the Sulimani family feel about your victory?" yelled another.

One bold reporter stepped forward, "Crown Attorney Kelly, congratulations on your win. Was it hard to try a case which involved a council member?" asked Paul Knight from the local television station, thrusting a microphone in Lily's face.

"Anyone who commits a crime in Happy Valley will be tried by the Crown with the full force of the law, despite their office. So no, I did not find it difficult to do my job," Lily replied testily.

"Thank you, Ms. Kelly. What does the Sulimani family think about the judgement?"

"Amani Sulimani was five years old, when Zebadiah Rockwood's truck went through a red light. His truck struck the back of the Sulimani's SUV killing her. He then left the scene pursued by good Samaritans, who wished to stop Mr. Rockwood from continuing driving drunk: a pursuit caused by Mr. Rockwood's actions, which put a number of lives in danger."

"Will the family be comforted with this conviction?" queried another reporter.

"Amani Sulimani existed as their only child. Mr. Rockwood's conviction will not bring her back, but hopefully will bring some peace of mind to her family knowing he will be behind bars." Lily answered.

"Do you sense, given your own personal tragedies that you'll be able to get a sentence fitting the crime?"

"My family's history does not come into my trial cases, only the person's guilt."

"And when will sentencing take place?" asked another reporter.

"Sentencing will take place next month."

"Thank you Ms. Kelly. This is Paul Knight reporting, with an update on the Zebadiah Rockwood's drunken driving case. Zebadiah Rockwood was a long time council member here in Happy Valley. He took a leave of absence to deal with his legal issues. Mr. Rockwood was charged with impaired driving causing death, two counts of failing to remain at the scene of an accident and dangerous driving last December. When asked about the conviction today Mr. Rockwood and his lawyer issued a no comment. We will have the complete story for you at six pm. Paul Knight reporting for *CHPV-TV*."

Lily hated speaking on camera, even though it was part of her job as the Crown attorney, so she was glad the scrum had been completed.

She hated sounding tough and unyielding but it was all in the description of her job title. She had fought difficult challenges to get this job and she had to work hard and fight hard to keep it. After all there were aspects of her job her she loved like putting the bad people that would harm others away. The press was gone and she was now free to go to her office to file her reports and leave early. She crossed the street, entered her building and went straight up to her office.

"Victory is mine!" Lily Kelly cried triumphantly as she walked into her office.

"So you won?" asked Colleen Finn, her administrative assistant.

"Yes, I bested that idiot, Michael Taylor. He thought he would beat me in court. He actually believed his client would win."

"Good for you, boss, I knew you would nail his lily white ass to the wall. He's such a scumbag lawyer all his clients seem to be as guilty as hell."

"Colleen! Language! But thank-you," Lily answered, showing pearly white teeth.

Colleen looked expectantly at Lily and she felt stupid did she miss something? Oh the joke! Lily hadn't laughed at Colleen's wit.

"Funny, I got it. Zebadiah Rockwood's sentencing takes place next month, but he will be held until then; no bail, no goodbyes to his favourite watering hole. As the Crown, I'll recommend the longest sentence I can get that he can serve. It's victories like these which make my job worthwhile. I don't know how much satisfaction this will give that little girl's family, but at least they'll know her killer remains in jail. He can't take another life again, because he will be incarcerated."

Lily went over to her desk and sat down.

"Can you imagine Michael Taylor, tried to use the defence that Rockwood was not drunk. Just tired? He claimed Rockwood drank only after the accident, while driving his company's truck; so the company couldn't possibly be responsible,"
"I believe you told me that before," Colleen commented, "However I'm glad you proved he'd drank so much before getting in the truck. That proved he was legally under the influence when the accident occurred. I hope I was some help in that aspect."
"Yes, you were invaluable."
"Thanks, Lily."
"It's still early; only nine forty-five, and my day's clear until what, two-thirty?"
"That's correct." Colleen replied.

Colleen checked a day planner, frowning, "Is everything okay, Lily? You seem a little down."

"Everything is fine. Amelia's grand opening starts at noon, but I promised to be there sooner if possible. If I go right now, I'll surprise her," Lily grabbed her coat to leave.

"I'm glad she's doing so well. Although after what happened, Amelia needs the encouragement. Please tell her, I'll try to get to her store another day. I hope her store has great success."

"Thank-you, I will tell Amelia. Hold all my calls Colleen. Unless it's urgent then call my cell."

"I'll do that. What time should I say you'll be back?" Colleen responded to a departing Lily.

"Tell whoever asks that I'll be back after two p.m..."

"And if they ask where you are?" Colleen questioned.

"Tell them I'm meeting with a witness," Lily replied with a wink.

"If there's cake bring me back a piece. Please, boss?" Colleen begged.

"I ordered a cake, but it's not supposed to arrive until one thirty so we'll see. I'm leaving now. Remember only urgent calls to my cell phone." Lily cautioned, leaving through the front door.

She twisted her shimmering brown hair back up into its traditional bun. Pulling out her cell phone, she dialled Amelia's store. There was no answer. How odd! Amelia must be busy putting out last minute stock.

~0~

A few minutes ago

Alone male walked into the store. His left hand held a gun while his right hand steadied it. He strode in with caution. His dark brown eyes dart from corner to corner, searching for an assailant. His well over six-foot tall frame slouched. Ruggedly handsome, with dark brown hair clipped short to his head; he was dressed in a dark blue jacket and dress pants; a badge is also clipped to his belt buckle. Finding the scene secure he putting his gun away and pulled a pair of gloves out of his suit coat pocket and a pair of booties, which he slipped on his shoes.

He checked the victim. No pulse. Advancing forward, he bent down to check the second woman; her phone still in her hand, her head bloody. He noted the second victim was still breathing, though unconscious. He looked around, as if waiting for someone. Deciding they weren't coming yet, he took out a mini recorder. He started scanning the scene and speaking aloud.

"This is Sergeant Detective Emmett Rogers. I am at the scene of a homicide, at Quirks, one forty five Maple Street. A woman lays sprawled out across the floor. The woman's arms are positioned underneath her, as if to break her fall. The back of her head and her long blonde hair are streaked in rusty-brown blood, as well as her clothing below the hair. Blood pools across the floor spiralling out in two long streams. Footprints are noticeable, as if someone stepped through the drying blood. The weapon appears to be a pair of scissors, found beneath the victim. I have marked both of these."

The man spoke aloud as he walked around, carefully avoiding contaminating the evidence, by stepping over a paper cup.

"A coffee cup... possibly one of those lattes is overturned. I'm sure the forensics team can determine this if necessary. Its contents are also spilled on the floor and countertop. Coffee is spilled at the front door and possibly on the shoes. The second victim's shoes are not on the bruised victim, but on the floor. The shoes can be found near an overturned ladder, at the front door. It appears the woman, who appears unconscious, may have been carrying a ladder and toy stock to place on the shelves, when she slipped in the blood.

The man paused to think.

"This might be a setup by the second victim to cover the actual crime. The woman, however, seems to have the victim's blood all over her clothes and hands like she crawled through the blood. I believe there are two possible scenarios here. One the owner of the shop, one Amelia Kelly (the unconscious person), murdered her employee or unknown victim and set this up to appear a perpetrator broke in and killed her accidentally hurting herself in the process. Or two... it is at it now seems that she stumbled on the crime scene and harmed herself."

He pulled out a notebook again and examined the room taking some more taking notes.

"Is it a robbery gone wrong? It is too soon to tell. The store owner will be en-route to hospital as soon as the EMTs have arrived. Interview to follow. The time is now ten twenty a.m.," he concluded turning off his recorder.
He examined the room scribbling on his notepad.

~0~

Now
Lily and Detective Emmett Rogers

T he man's eyes turn and his vision focused completely.

A woman entered the store. His eyes took in her tall and slender form and her long shimmering brown hair, pulled into a tight roll. He noted she was closely followed by the Emergency technicians and gave a sigh of relief. The woman entering the store had brilliant blue eyes. He had a feeling she often turned heads, even dressed as she was, in her business attire. But he noted something about the way she walked screamed money and upper class.

"Oh no, Amelia!" she screamed and tried to rush to Amelia, but was stopped by the man's arm.
"This is a crime scene ma'am. We don't want you disrupting our evidence. Let the EMTs and detectives do their job. Then you can go to ...you're er...friend?" Sergeant Detective Rogers commanded.
"Crime scene? What has happened?" Lily asked politely, wanting to be cooperative.

"Ma'am, I'll know better after I assess the scene. Until then, please remain near the front door." ordered Detective Rogers briskly.

"I promise I'll stay out of the way; but at least can I get her Adrienne Changs?"

"What or who, are Adrienne Changs?" said Detective Rogers looking totally perplexed.

"Shoes, those shoes right there!" Lily pointed to a pair of heels lying behind the yellow tape.

"You're worried about shoes? Woman! Do you have any idea of what's going on here?" Detective Rogers snapped, shaking his head.

"You sexist pig!" countered Lily under her breath, "Men!" Losing her temper now and louder she continued, "Those shoes are worth five hundred dollars! And she probably wore them for what a half an hour? And you want me to walk away and leave them to be destroyed in some kind of liquid!"

"Liquid that's blood! And five hundred dollars for shoes? Is she crazy?" Detective Rogers asked dumfounded.

"No! She's not crazy. How dare you?" Lily asked suddenly outraged.

He was smug wasn't he? Handsome yes, but oh so smug, she questioned herself. That wasn't important. Amelia was injured on the floor and he questioned her? Instead of letting her go to her cousin! What was wrong with Lily? Why was she so worried and focused on the shoes? They were only shoes. Amelia was injured; who cared about footwear?

"Sorry, ma'am, the shoes are evidence now. Name? Occupation? Address?" Detective Rogers barked, ignoring her statement.

"I want to see your identification first, and then you'll get the information," insisted Lily.

"I am Sergeant Detective Emmett Rogers," the man revealed, showing his police badge.

"Oh that's funny," Lily uttered laughing, "If you and Amelia were introduced it would be Aem and Em."

Lily followed this up by hysterically laughing and then alternatively crying. What was wrong with her? She never lost it like this. She always appeared a professional. She had seen crime scenes. She could handle this. Couldn't she? Amelia would be okay. Wouldn't she?!

Get a hold of yourself Lily. You have embarrassed yourself! Lily heard this voice in her head, she recognized as her father's. Odd how her Dad's voice, came back to her now, she rarely saw him, since he lived in Prague and he only called about twice a year.

"Ma'am, what you are saying is not remotely funny. Are you all right? Put your head between your knees if you feel lightheaded. I think your friend's relatively fine. She might have a head injury and possibly a broken leg, but she'll be okay." Sergeant Detective Rogers then turned to the Emergency technicians (EMTs) to seek confirmation demanded ,"Right?"

"Should be. But head injuries can be serious," the one EMT replied.

Sergeant Detective Rogers shot him a disapproving look.

"Yes, the Sergeant Detective is right. She'll be fine. She'll be taken to the hospital for treatment," the Emergency Technician agreed, finally.

"See...what did I tell you? Now that we have that out of the way; I need to see some identification and then get some answers to my questions. Name? Address? Occupation? The reason you are here?" Detective Rogers barked at Lily.

"Amelia's my best friend and more. This should have been the greatest day of her life, her opening of her new store; a one of kind toy and collectibles retailer. A grand opening and now it's ruined. Who did this to her?" Lily asked, uncharacteristically wringing her hands and still trying to regain her calm, as thoughts of Amelia's demise threatened to enter her mind.

"Ma'am, she slipped in blood. She hit her head on the floor and on the ladder. No one harmed her. She did this to herself," explained Sergeant Detective Rogers.

"I realize she's clumsy, but she didn't put blood there to trip in," defended Lily angrily.

"No, the blood was spilled by whoever killed the woman behind the counter."

"Someone is dead behind the counter?" Lily responded shocked and surprised.

"No comment; as I explained Ma'am this is an active crime scene. Now as I asked before what is your name?" Detective Rogers insisted forcefully again.

"Lily Kelly-Brooksfield. My husband is Horace Brooksfield, the mayor. We live down the street on Beaconfield. Do you want the number? It's nine hundred and sixty-two." she replied condescendingly.

"If you're Mayor Brooksfield's wife... then you're the Crown Attorney." Coming to this realization, Sergeant Detective Rogers hid a sigh.

"Please update me on this active crime scene, now," commanded Lily pulling back her shoulders.

Emmett Rogers put on his professional face and smiled. The smile was just so warm and inviting that Lily felt warm all over. Lily frowned back at him; she was just felt so angry. This cop who grinned back at her was the biggest reason. She was a married woman. She shouldn't be attracted to a cop who apparently existed to give her grief and solve a murder. She threw back her shoulders again. It was okay to look at someone attractive, she excused herself. Everyone looks, and most of the time it meant nothing. It's only if you acted on any attraction it became wrong. She would never act on the temptation. Besides he appeared to be the most annoying man she'd ever met.

"Ma'am, you know I can't fill you in on any of this case. You'll have to recuse yourself from this case, as you're familiar with the crime scene." Detective Rogers emphasized, once again interrupting Lily's thoughts.

"Why don't you just come out and say what you think. You consider me a suspect," Lily uttered.

"A lot of people are suspects in my book. I have to make a case for them committing the crime or I have to eliminate them as suspects. And don't attempt to solve this yourself; amateurs just get in the way." Detective Rogers explained, his eyes wandering.

Lily was slightly amused. Detective Rogers thought she wanted to insinuate herself into this murder investigation? She might not have before that comment, but she did now. He seemed to be focusing on Amelia or Lily as his prime suspect. Lily knew neither of them had committed this murder, so that meant she had no choice but to find out for herself who had committed this crime. She would pretend she wanted nothing to do with this situation, even as far as passing it off to her underling Barbara. After all she could always investigate behind the scenes.

Spotting the emergency technicians Detective Rogers exclaimed "Oh good, the ambulance has arrived to take the victim to the hospital. Now can we can get down to brass tacks; you can fill me in on these people and anything else you know or have held back from me."

"I want to go with her," Lily protested.

Lily pulled herself back taking several steps back putting distance between herself and this cop. It was odd, how alive she felt when she jousted with him. He was a cop investigating a murder and she was married.

Stop this now Lily! She told herself.

"Ma'am, I realize you want to go see your friend. Before I could release you from the scene, I need something from you. We need you to identify the other victim. Maybe you'll recognize her when I turn over the body." Detective Rogers explained, softening a little, as he slipped on another pair of gloves.

"Only if you'll stop calling me Ma'am. Call me Lily or Crown Attorney Kelly, but not Ma'am. It makes me feel eighty years old."

"If it will get you to identify the victim...thank-you Crown Attorney Kelly."

"Let's look, shall we?" Lily agreed.

Lily took a breath as she gathered herself to observe who lay there dead. She gasped as she stared over the counter to see the back of the woman's head. She covered her mouth in horror.

"Good grief! I never realized they appear so alike from the back," replied Lily shocked.

"Who do you think she looks like ma'am?" demanded Detective Rogers.

"What did I say about ma'am? Don't they give you sensitivity training at Police College? You want to know who this is? This is Megan, Megan Fowler. She's an employee of Amelia's. But she works evenings she's...is....was a college student. I can't believe this is Megan. Megan is such a sweet girl and worked part-time to be able to go to school and support her mother. Why would someone kill her? Do you think it's possible someone mistook her for Amelia?" Lily rambled, tears slipping from her eyes.

"That's a possibility, ma'am. We will explore all aspects."

"I know the drill, Sergeant Detective Rogers." Lily gave the detective a mock salute, "Why can't you admit that they mistook Megan for Amelia?"

"We don't have any of the facts yet, Ms. Kelly," replied Detective Rogers.

"What about Amelia? Is she in any danger?" asked Lily. "If I were to speculate, I suppose that could be a possibility," Detective Rogers answered non-committally.

They both watched as the technicians gathered the evidence and blood samples and took pictures before the body was taken away.

"Will someone be assigned to guard her and keep her safe?" Lily asked getting exasperated.

"That's in motion, Crown Attorney Kelly," Detective Rogers explained, trying not to sound annoyed that she's telling him how to do his job.

Detective Rogers and Lily turned as another cop swaggered into the store. Burly and well over six feet tall, his hair was dark like Detective Rogers. Unlike Detective Rogers, this man preened like a peacock; Lily was aware of the type. Guys like him smiled with their mouths and not their eyes. They thought all women should admire them and only them. She noted his smile went as far as his lips.

"What have you got here, Emmett?"

"Nothing you need to be concerned about, Brad," Detective Rogers replied, obvious tension showing between the two.

"You should be able to get some great publicity out of this one," Brad said loudly to Detective Rogers.

Brad then strutted over to the murder scene.

"It's my case, Brad," Detective Rogers insisted.

"I'm not trying to interfere," Brad persisted walking around, "I just thought if you needed some help I would lend a hand. It doesn't look like something you could handle on your own."

"I don't need help, thanks, Brad. I don't need you messing up my crime scene." Detective Rogers declared "I've got it all under control.

"It doesn't look that way to me. I would solve this case quickly. You could use me in your corner," Brad continued.

"We don't need you. Now the Crown attorney is here, so I have it all in hand. Goodbye, Brad." Detective Rogers practically spat.

"Ah, the lovely Crown attorney Kelly is here. Can't go now," Brad exclaimed trying to sound charming but failing miserably.

"And you are?" asked Lily putting her full aristocratic chill in to her voice.

"I'm Brad Owens, at your service, Attorney Kelly. Sergeant Detective Brad Owens. I use to be Emmett's partner," Brad explained smiling and pointing to Detective Rogers.

Detective Rogers rolled his eyes. "Thank God you're not anymore," He stated under his breath loud enough for only he and Lily to hear.

"So what do you think, Crown Attorney? Was it a robbery gone wrong?" asked Brad.

"I'm not sure. Why do I bother to tell you this? This isn't your case," Lily commented suddenly not willing to share with Brad.

She didn't know why. Something about his smile, and the way Emmett Rogers had reacted to him made her dislike him. Brad's smile was phony, like a used car salesman. It was slick and slimy. That wasn't fair to used car sales people. Lily was sure they were more honest than this phoney, Brad Owens. Lily had come across a lot of people in her job. She certainly felt she was a good judge of character. In fact, she could spot a phoney a mile away. Detective Emmett Rogers, unlike Brad Owens, appeared like he knew his job. She'd heard of him many times, but had never run into him on the job until today. Thank goodness for the Internet on her phone. He was a dedicated cop. He had done his time and had come up through the ranks, strictly on merit. Detective Rogers didn't seem to like Brad Owens and that was reason enough for Lily not to trust him.

Emmett Rogers had an exemplary record as a police officer; she trusted his instincts and knowledge over this smarmy, Detective Brad Owens. He'd get to the bottom of this. Lily wished he would let her leave soon and check on Amelia. They had spent their teen years together and were as close as sisters. She'd always felt responsible for Amelia, being two years older. She wanted to make sure Amelia was okay.

"Okay. Well if you don't need my help, I'm leaving because I have work to do. There are other crimes to investigate." Brad answered leaving, "See you around Emmett."
"Not if I see you first," muttered Emmett under his breath.
"So am I free to go?" Lily demanded.

Emmett then offered her his pen.

"I have your address, so as long as you sign here in my notebook. "You are free to go," he said gesturing.

Lily glanced over at Detective Owens and watched him leave before reaching for the book. She then signed her signature with a flourish. Detective Rogers scanned the signature, thinking momentarily it was just as elegant as Lily. He shook his head, reminding himself to stay connected to reality.

"So I am free to go, Detective?" Lily repeated.
"I'll be checking in on your friend, of course, and I may need to follow-up with you later, but as of now, you are free to go." he smiled, already exhausted.
"I would expect nothing else from you, Detective Rogers."

As she got into her car, Lily breathed a sigh of relief she had finally been able to leave the store. She buckled up her seatbelt and put her car in gear.

Backing the car up, Lily pulled out into the street and narrowly missed getting hit by a car, she didn't view. Luckily the other driver slammed on his brakes. She noticed the male driver shouting, "Stupid woman driver" as she read his lips in her rear view mirror. He was justified in his anger. It had been her fault, but she didn't have time to dwell.

She headed down the road toward the hospital; despite her resolve her mind wandered. She thought about poor Megan's mother getting the news of her daughter's death. It would kill Lily to get news like that about her adopted daughter, Rose. What kind of monster kills a young woman? Why did, whomever it was, have to kill Megan? It wasn't a robbery, she'd read in Detective Rogers' notes, when he gave his notebook to her to sign her statement. As Lily drove, more questions flooded into her head. Was Amelia the real target? Megan certainly appeared like Amelia from the back.

Amelia didn't appear too hurt. Maybe she suffered a concussion? Concussions could be serious; she knew from her readings. The EMT hadn't said Amelia was in serious condition though. Not that the EMT could explain before Emmett Rogers got on his case. Revving the engine, she waited impatiently for the light to go green. Once Lily reached the hospital, she could reassure herself, Amelia was all right.

~0~

*Please continue reading an excerpt from **A Diller A Dollar A Really Dead Scholar.***

Excerpt From~ A Diller A Dollar A Really Dead Scholar-Chapter 1 - Real Life Is Worse than a Movie

'A diller, a dollar, A ten o'clock scholar; What makes you come so soon? You used to come at ten o'clock, But now you come at noon!' ~Nursery Rhyme, Author Unknown

Rose

Rose arrived early for choir with Carol, by her side.

She wasn't aware of what she would have done without her constant side kick, and best friend Carol in the last few weeks. Carol had amazingly defended her making her proud to be her friend. However, the calendar said the second week of school and the whispers still continued. Gossip was continually passed around about the murders but especially at school.

Rose was tired of all of the innuendoes and speculation, she thought. Her father had died, no not simply died; he had been murdered by a serial killer. This should have garnered some sympathy, for both the circumstances of her father's death, and the manner, but all she caught was jokes about the position he had been found.

Rose guessed finding him naked with his secretary; who he'd been having an affair with led to the gossip, but she was so tired of all of it. If that wasn't bad enough though, everyone had to find out this serial killer had killed many people. He had killed Rose's Great Uncle Jerry, Aunt Aerilla, and her cousins Robert and Grace before Aunt Amelia came to Happy Valley. Last year he had murdered Aunt Amelia's husband Jack and killed her little boy Sam. Continuing on his killing spree, he had killed Aunt Amelia's employee Megan and the homeless guy Mr. Young. All of this simply because he was obsessed, horribly obsessed with Aunt Amelia, all of so senseless and stupid. She grew tired of talking about the incident.

Who did she kid? She couldn't even talk about her father's death to the shrink, her mother made her visit. People came up to her at school and wanted gruesome details. Or they wanted to know more about the capture of the serial killer. Grandma Katha called him the cop in wolf's clothing, and some other names Rose didn't care to repeat. She wanted to scream. Torn Rose hated and loved Happy Valley, Ontario, both at the same time. It was after all the place she was born, but the buildings were old here and the town was dying as prosperity had flown along, with a number of businesses that employed people. Would there even be a job for Rose when she wanted one? With the loss of jobs, people's attitudes had changed or maybe they'd just revealed themselves to be small minded and frankly she was tired of it. As soon as she could she was going away to university and then she'd live in another city when she graduated, visiting Lily, Grandma Katha and Amelia regularly.

Rose just wanted to be Rose Brooksfield again...not Rose Brooksfield whose father had been murdered. Wasn't it bad enough that Her mother Lily Brooksfield, or Lily Kelly as she had always called herself, Mom now dated the cop, who had investigated her Dad's murder.
What did it mean about Mom's true feelings for her Dad, Horace, that she had moved on so quickly? Rose had encouraged Mom, but she had been rash. Mom should be thinking of her Dad not this Emmett Rogers all the time.

Now all Rose ever heard from Mom was Emmett this and Emmett that. What about Dad had she forgotten him? And if she had forgotten him... what did that mean for Rose? After all she was Lily's adopted daughter not her flesh and blood. If Mom got married to Emmett, would there be room for Rose? What would happen if Mom decided to have children with Emmett? Rose bit her lip she had to stop thinking this way as Grandma Katha declared this borrowed trouble, but still Rose worried.

Rose looked over at Carol as she flicked her long blonde hair out of her eyes. Rose thought that Carol dying her hair blonder had made Carol's eyes look bluer and her fair skin even more ivory looking. Carol seemed to be getting a lot more looks from guys too. What was up with that? Maybe Rose should cut her long hair? She didn't want to look exactly like her best friend from the back. Maybe she should make her hair reddish brown like her mom, Lily's. Then they'd be more alike, with hair and eyes matching in colour.

Rose suddenly looked up from her thoughts as she noticed the light bulb appeared out in the hallway near the gym. How odd she thought she wished the janitor would change the bulb quickly. It was creepy here at six a.m., even with Carol at her side. As they reached the choir room, Rose was relieved to find the light on in the room. But where was Mr. Scholar the choir teacher?

"I don't understand why Mr. Scholar called a six-thirty a.m. practice and can't be here when we get to the room," complained Carol loudly.

When Rose didn't answer right away she whined. "Aren't you talking to me yet?"

"I had to catch my breath, besides my leg hurts and I have a cramp in my leg. All the fast cycling on my bike pulled a muscle or something in my leg, and now my stomach hurts."

"Why don't you walk around the room and get rid of your cramp? I'm going to sit here and snooze. Wake me up when someone comes. I don't want anyone to catch me sleeping," Carol replied.

Rose walked around the room. The cramp in her leg, didn't seem to ease and neither did her stomach cramp. Rose's shoe slipped and she surprised herself, stepping into something sticky in a dark corner of the room. Great, now something was on my brand new shoes. Icky she thought. She glanced down, that looked like blood. It couldn't be? Could it? Did someone get a nose bleed, perhaps Mr. Scholar?

She peered behind the desk looking for the source of the blood and saw to her great shock Mr. Scholar lay dead. A knife protruded in the place where his heart should have been. Rose stared for a moment, not believing what her eyes saw. How could Mr. Scholar be lying dead, his chest bared open and nothing inside of him.

It seemed so unreal, like one of those movies she watched at Anna's. If her mother had known she viewed a chop movie, Rose would be in so much trouble. As it is she'd observed the movie with her hands over her eyes but this.... This was real....Mr. Scholar had obviously been murdered brutally murdered and his organs were gone. Was it his heart? Because Rose was sure that's where the teacher had declared it was in biology. Oh my God, what if the killer was still nearby? Rose scanned the room with her eyes seeking out all the spaces in the room where someone may hide. How could Carol be sitting dozing in a chair? Carol slept waiting for the choir teacher, while he lay dead near her.

"Rose what's wrong with you? Why did you gasp?" asked Carol, waking up and noticing Rose stillness and alarm at the same time.

"Carol he's dead," Rose indicated.

"I appreciate your dad is dead and we are all sad, but why bring that up now Rose?" Carol retorted exasperated.

"Mr. Scholar is here."

"I don't see him."

"That's because he's behind the desk. He's dead," Rose replied in a whisper.

"What did he have a heart attack or something? He's awful young for that, but I understand lots of people have sudden heart attacks," rambled Carol.

"Carol can you be quiet?"

"Well good grief, blame me like that it's not my fault the guy decided to have a heart attack!"

"He didn't have a heart attack, someone has killed him and I think they took his heart."

"Don't joke around Rose. It isn't funny."

"I'm not joking."

"Oh my God and we're still in this room alone. The killer could come back and get us, if he isn't in here all ready. I want my mother!" wailed Carol texting on her cell phone and getting no answer.

"We have to get out of here. People should be in the Gym, this time of morning they practice for basketball." Rose replied thinking on her feet, "I want my mom, too."

"Call her. Call your mother. Ask her what to do! She's always got an answer," demanded Carol.

"Let's lock the door first and put a chair in front of it. No one is in here now, but they might have a key for all we know."

"I did that already. I'm calling my Mom," stated Rose dialling.

"Mommy...,"cried Rose, as Lily answered.

"What is wrong Rose? What has happened?" demanded Lily.

"Mommy," Rose began incoherently through sobs.

"Take a deep breath now. Speak slowly and clearly. Tell your mother what is wrong," demanded Lily.

"Mr. Scholar the choir teacher is dead," Rose told her through the sobs.

"What? Did he have a heart attack? Are you okay? Of course, you're not okay. Do you want me to come to the school, baby? I can be there in ten minutes." Lily exclaimed quickly.

"Mommy he's bee....nnn he's bee....nnn mur...dered. Someone took his heart I think," Rose hiccupped.

"What? Who is with you? Are you safe?" demanded Lily.

"No one's here. It's just me and Carol. We are so scared, mom. I want you here."

"It will be okay baby, tell me everything, but first is the room safe you're in? Is it locked, and blocked?"

"Yes, we locked the door and blocked the door as well for now, but I don't want to stay here Mommy. It's icky and the killer might come back."

"What did she say? What did she say we should do?" demanded Carol.

"Quiet. I want to understand what my Mom said," implored Rose to Carol, and then speaking to Lily she replied.

"Sorry, go ahead mom."

"So tell me what happened," Lily demanded.

"I had a cramp in my leg, because I rode my bike to school fast. We raced then I won. I didn't see Mr. Scholar at first. I walked over near his desk and slipped in something sticky. Mommy, his blood is all over my new shoes. It's all over my shoes!" Rose answered in horror.

"Then what did you see?" prompted Lily trying to calm her daughter.

"I saw him. His chest is wide open and it is empty. There's nothing there, but tons of blood around and in him. I think his heart is gone. A knife is stuck in his chest," Rose sputtered a torrent of words, tumbling out of her.

"Okay, here is what I need you both to do to do. First, did Carol get near the body, or step in the blood?" demanded Lily.

"No. Lucky girl, Carol's shoes are fine. Mine are a total loss."

"Okay, did you track much blood, across the floor?" inquired Lily "And does the door own a lock that you can turn?"

"Blood?" Rose asked shock setting it as she stared at her shoes.

"Focus, Rose. I know it's difficult but you need to focus."

"Okay. Yes, we blocked the door I did track blood across the floor, since I had my shoes on, and yes the lock turns and then you can shut it behind you."

"Okay then carefully. Now take off your shoes and leave them on the floor. Be careful to walk only where blood isn't in your sock feet," Lily advised. "Walking to the door, I want you unblock the entrance, and then run don't walk, where people congregate. Also remain on the phone until you observe lots of people. Then take Carol's phone, while you still talking to me and call the police."

"I will Mom. We will run to the gym. They practice basketball there, early in the mornings."

Rose and Carol then flew down the hall and burst into the gym.

"Ladies, we are practice basketball here, would you like a detention?" shouted the coach.

"There's been a murder and we want to be with people," Carol shouted back belligerently.

"Carol Banks, if you made up something...,"threatened the coach as he then saw Rose who spoke into Carol's cell phone.

"911. How can I direct your call?" asked the Operator 'Fire? Ambulance? Police?"

"Police, please?" Rose demanded, as she felt an eerie calm come over herself and heard herself give the details from far away.

"There's been a murder at Happy Valley High school. It's the choir teacher Mr. Scholar. He's been murdered in the choir room with a knife. Oh no, I sound like a clue game and it's not funny. It's horrible! He's dead," Rose stated horrified, a chill coming over her. Rose suddenly felt light-headed, and with blurry vision, quickly fell to the gym floor.

~0~

Look for Emmett and Lily further adventures and the rest of the Clan Kelly's fun in Book 2 of the Kelly Murder Mysteries - A Diller a Dollar a Real Dead Scholar, on sale now in e-book soon in paperback. If you enjoyed this book please consider leaving me a few words at your favourite retailer. Please continuing reading on for an excerpt from **Dreams Can Kill.**

Sincerely S. G. Lee

~0~

Excerpt from ~ Dreams Can Kill-Chapter 1 - Survival

The rain pelted down on me, as I struggled to come to my senses. My head felt like it had split in two, as if little lumberjacks had taken up residence. I opened one eye. The world spun sideways like a ride at the fair. I tried shutting one eye, then the other. I nearly fell back to sleep. I opened my eyes again, fighting the sleep which wanted to overtake me. I shuttered my eyes again, as my stomach protested. My whole body manipulated, bruised, bent and broken like some old rag doll discarded.

Sleep...sleep would solve my problems, my brain protested. No! I had a reason I needed to stay awake and alert...A little sleep, a part of me protested again. No, I must stay conscious. But I remained so tired. I dragged myself across the pebbled ground. My right leg stuck out at an impossible angle, obviously broken. I saw by lifting my head slightly and turning it that there appeared to be a road up ahead. I had to get to the road. If I dragged myself that far, surely I would be rescued?

But it was oh so hard, to drag yourself backwards, when you couldn't perceive where you were going. Oh no, what if he came back. He would finish me off...finish what he had started.

He who? Who was this person, who left me to die? Why couldn't I remember? Don't panic… the thing to do is right now is to reach help; then and only then would I be safe. I caressed large pieces of gravel which cut into the back of my head. I sensed I was close to the road. I reached out with my good hand and touched a paved surface. I knew I didn't have much strength left. I experienced the energy drain quickly leaving my body. I tried to fight the drain, but the world faded to black.

~0~

If you like to read more of this book or any of my other books they are available in paperback or kindle at Amazon.
Sincerely S. G. Lee